TRUST DANNY JAMES

MAX DELANEY

IRONTREE PUBLICATIONS

An IRONTREE publication

ONE

THE FALL

DANNY JAMES CLICKED the mouse button and immediately regretted it. In that moment he knew his world had ended.

Before he could stop it, the CD tray jerked violently out of the computer. The desk wobbled, and the vase he had just put down started to rock back and forth. Danny watched as the white china vase, with its tiny hand-painted birds, slowly began to tip over. Then, with a sudden sense of doom, he realised that his mother's favourite vase was now falling rapidly towards the back of his desk and the open window. The colourful little birds spun away in a blur of blue and orange and then disappeared from view as the vase plummeted down towards the ground below.

Danny glared at the space where the vase had been. Then his eyes darted to the window.

He cursed quietly, leaned over his desk and looked

out. He was almost too afraid of what he would see, but he had to know. Scanning the ground far below him, Danny wondered why he hadn't heard a crash. Why aren't there any bits of broken vase down there? After a moment he remembered…

"The ivy," he pulled at a few leaves just below his window and then poked his head out further. There, he spotted a bright glint of white china nestling in the ivy halfway down the wall.

"Saved," he muttered. His mum's vase was safe, and so was his skin. But, now what… How to get the lucky ornament back inside?

A fishing rod? He didn't have one that worked.

A piece of string and some blue tack? That seemed a bit too unreliable.

A net… Did he have a net? Not in his room? Did he have one in the garage - or was it still packed away somewhere after the house move?

The thoughts came thick and fast. Danny had dozens of different ideas… However, he acted on the only one which seemed necessary.

The simplest and most obvious idea would be the best.

With a quick jump, he was sitting on the back of his desk. Then a push and he was halfway through the window, arms hanging down. The vase, sadly, remained just out of reach.

A moment later he was lying on his stomach, half out of the window. That was better… closer. He wriggled forwards, risking more of his body outside. Closer, only a fingertip away now. He wriggled again.

Only his legs remained in the room, the rest of his body was tipped out. With his arms outstretched, he was as close as he could be to reaching the vase.

At that moment, he sensed a sound behind him in his bedroom. The door had been violently flung open, and his sister's shocked voice called out: "Danny, what on Earth are you doing?"

"I'm okay," he called back. But he wasn't.

The action of moving to look over his shoulder had caused him to slip forwards. Now he was overbalancing and starting to fall forwards. All at once, the air swooped around his ears, and he felt himself rushing headlong towards the floor. It seems a long way down. He sensed his slippers catching on the old wooden window sill, and his left slipper was knocked off. It flew over him in a wonderfully curved arc.

His body flipped over in a far more clumsy way. Instinctively he was grabbing for something to save him, at first it was only air, which wasn't particularly useful. Then his fingers caught hold of something soft and waxy. He realised he had managed to grip onto a good handful of strong ivy leaves. The same ivy which had saved the vase.

He was moving too fast, and he tumbled over like an acrobat doing a backflip onto a Gym mat. The only differences were that Danny was not a skilled acrobat, and the paved driveway beneath him offered a most unwelcoming landing site. He was gripping the ivy so firmly, however, that it managed to stage his fall. And the next few events happened in a series of little accidents: his back hit the wall with a thud, the ivy tore apart, and he dropped the last few feet to the floor.

Danny landed in a heap on his stomach, handfuls of torn ivy leaves in each hand. He could tell his knees and elbows had received some painful scratches, and there seemed to be a particularly jagged stone digging into his chest. He managed to roll awkwardly onto his side. A few seconds later, just as he was getting comfortable with the idea of still being alive, something gently landed on his stomach. The vase, suddenly released from the safety of the ivy, fell on top of him, bounced, and then hit the floor.

"Oh no!" he managed to groan as he turned to look.

The world was a dizzy flash of colours for a moment. When the fuzzy special effects settled down, he could see his mum's most beloved ornament was laying at the side of him on the floor.

He counted at least five pieces.

TWO
RUSHING INTO THINGS

DANNY STUMBLED TO HIS FEET. His jeans were torn and there seemed to be blood on the arms of his shirt. What worried him most though was what remained on the floor. He picked up the pieces of the vase, cradled them in his hands and headed towards the kitchen. Just as he got close the door opened and his sister stormed out.

"Danny, what were you doing?" She looked him up and down.

He grinned: "I wasn't flying, that's for sure." Then he grimaced as the pain in his knees returned.

"Are you alright?"

Danny was touched that her concern seemed real. His sister was a few years older than him, and that gap meant that there tended to be a cool sense of acceptance between them rather than any true friendship.

"You should be careful," Ellie continued. "Why were you hanging out of the…" She stopped abruptly and looked at the remains of the vase in his hands. "Is that Mum's?"

"It was."

"What were you doing?"

"I was looking at it and…" Danny pulled back from the explanation to ask urgently: "Where is Mum?"

"Don't worry, she's in the study. Preparing for work…" Ellie said. Then she shrugged and added, "Of course!" Their mum spent a great deal of time at work, and when she wasn't at work, she was usually at home, preparing for the time when she would be back at work again.

"And Dad?"

"Don't worry," Ellie said again. "He's unpacking boxes in the dining room, so come on…" She grabbed his shoulder, "Let's try and sort this out."

They went into the kitchen. Ellie dampened some kitchen roll for the small cuts on his hands. Danny didn't seem to mind the cuts, he was too busy staring around the room. His mind was still dazed from the fall. When he first got up, an idea had hit him, but now it was hiding. What was it he'd thought of? He looked around:

His coat hung on the peg near the back door, was he going to escape?

The kettle? Was he going to make his mum a nice cup of tea and then tell her what happened?

The door to the cellar? Hide down there until everyone had worried about him and then he would reappear and they would be so pleased to see him they would forgive him anything?

The breadboard? Rush outside with it and… and what?

The kitchen cupboard? Glue!

That was it! It was obvious. He placed the bits of vase carefully beside the kettle and threw open the cupboard under the sink and started his hunt. There were hundreds of bottles in there. A bottle of stuff for cleaning wood, another for vinyl, one for kitchen work-tops and one for bathroom worktops. Three bottles were for cleaning windows. When did anyone ever clean windows? No good, only rubbish in that cupboard.

He moved to the next set of cupboards. Here was more stuff nobody ever used: a box of baking equip-ment, four flasks and a shelf full of paper plates marked "Happy 6th Birthday". No one was 6 anymore! As far as he knew, no one had been 6 for years. Oh, why was everything in the wrong place?

He pulled out a bag full of plastic bags and an old tin of fly spray. Then gave up on the cupboards.

Next, he started hunting through the kitchen draw-ers. When he got to the fourth drawer, he found what he wanted. It was a plastic packet of Ape-Man Glue, hidden behind some old keys and a broken potato peeler (why were they keeping that?). 'Ape-Man Glue, the quickest drying, most secure glue on Earth.' He read the words the advertising people had decided to write all over the front of the package. Great. This would solve everything.

He started to tear into the packet, but Ellie put out her hand to stop him. "I could have told you where that was if you'd asked," she said. "But you can't glue it here, anyway. Come on, you need to do this calmly and slowly. Think about it. Don't rush."

Danny was about to offer a rude reply, but he held back. Ellie filled the silence with more advice: "You're always charging about from one thing to the next. No wonder you have so many of these..." She seemed to have difficulty finding the right word. "These... accidents. Yes, Mum is right. You need to slow down. Focus. Think first. Remember what you're doing. Don't rush into things."

Danny was still a little dizzy from the fall and all the running around and searching. He could tell her a great deal about 'rushing into things', like the horrible way his family had rushed into the house move. Uprooting him from his wonderful home in Hanwell and all his friends. How they had been all been dragged out of London to this damp little village in Wales, without anyone asking him what he felt about it. Oh, he had a lot to say about 'rushing into things', but he kept quiet. Danny knew he needed to keep his sister on his side.

"Oh, I guess so," he said simply.

Then, with a sudden idea borrowed from his dad's sales talks, he managed to add: "You're right." That was hard to say, but needs must. "Will you help me with this, please? I thought we could glue the vase together. It's only five or six big bits." Danny added a faint smile. Perhaps all his injuries and a kind smile might make his sister like him for a bit longer.

"Come on then." Ellie took on the big-sister role happily. "You focus on what you are doing, and I'll help."

It seemed to Danny that she had suddenly become the person who would do anything to help her little brother. He liked that. He needed that right now.

As DANNY HEADED SLOWLY up the stairs, Ellie waited in the kitchen for a moment. The shock of falling out of the window had changed him, she thought. He was suddenly being quite sensible.

Once he had gone, she listened to the room. The kitchen was calm and quiet, with only the hum of the refrigeration to break the silence. She liked this place. Everything was peaceful. The house was old, and there was the smell of damp in some of the rooms, but it was a beautiful place. If the calm of the town and the surrounding hillside helped the whole family to chill, so much the better.

Her phone buzzed.

William had sent her a photo message. It was a selfie of him with his brother, Luke. They were fishing together.

Ah, William. That was another plus point for moving here: she'd met William!

She looked at the image again. The picture of Luke gave her an idea. She smiled quietly to herself. This would solve everything, she thought as she started to text a message to William.

A voice called from upstairs, it was Danny, managing the difficult trick of shouting loud enough to reach her but quiet enough so he wouldn't disturb Dad: "Ellie, are you coming?"

"I'm on my way," she said, still texting.

"Good, can you bring the glue? I left it down there?"

"Danny!"

THREE
ONE OF A PAIR

THEY WERE IN HIS BEDROOM, unopened boxes were piled everywhere from the house move. All of the rooms of the house were similar, but Danny's bedroom seemed to be the one filled with the most boxes. Ellie was sitting on one box with a taped down label which said, 'Books', Danny was on the end of his bed.

Ellie held the pieces of the vase in place while Danny looked to see if there were any gaps in the pattern. In places the scraps of china fitted together well, leaving only a hairline crack. Unfortunately, there were other sections where the pieces didn't match at all.

"Mum will be cross." Ellie said, "No matter how you glue this it's not going to look right."

"Of course she'll be cross, this was her favourite," Danny said gloomily. "You know when we moved house, she wrapped this vase in tons of bubble wrap.

She even put it in a box inside another box to protect it. She's always loved this one."

"So you threw it out of the window?"

Danny glared at her. He had the glue bottle in his hand and for a moment wondered if their new friendship should stop right there. For a split second, he was pouring it over Ellie's fantastically manicured fingernails… but he held back.

"It's for Mum's birthday next week," he explained. "According to Dad, because I've left Primary school I'm old enough to buy her a present with my own money. I thought I'd get her another vase."

Ellie was staring hard at him, "So, to make it really special, you thought you would smash this one?"

Danny tried to turn one of the vase fragments around to see if it fitted a space better. "This vase is one of a pair. I want to buy her the other one. See…" he pointed helpfully at the online shop's website on his computer. "I was comparing this vase to the one on the internet to make sure it matched."

Ellie considered this for a few moments and then nodded. She carefully jiggled four pieces of vase together while Danny tried to place the last one correctly. For the next few minutes, they worked together to recreate the vase from the jigsaw of odd shaped bits of china. It dawned on Danny after a while that he may have left a few tiny pieces down on the drive, but they managed to fill some of the smaller gaps with glue. "I don't need it to look perfect," he said as they capped the glue bottle and placed the repaired vase on his desk.

"It's a good job you don't need it to be perfect," Ellie said as she looked at their handiwork. "It's not."

Danny looked too. He had to agree. Although he was skilled in many areas, repairing china was not one of them. The cracks and breaks were particularly obvious. One of the little birds had lost a wing, and somehow another one had three legs. "It may look better when the glue dries," he said.

"Danny, it's no good. You'll have to buy her one to replace this one!"

He shook his head and pointed to the computer screen. The vases were £45 each. "I can't. I only have enough to buy one."

Danny switched off the computer. "It was Dad's fault, you know. He chose this awful machine. It's so bad it makes the desk shake." Danny stopped. It was his dad's fault for buying him a cheap computer with a CD tray that shot out like an alarmed rabbit whenever you ejected a disk. A more expensive machine would have glided open slowly on a cushion of oil. That would have given him time to catch the vase, and none of this would have happened.

Ellie reached out a hand and tapped the desk, it wobbled. She tugged at one of its legs, it wobbled even more. "It's not the computer. You never built this properly, did you?"

Danny sighed. "I was in a—"

"Hurry!"

"You can't blame me?" Even as he was saying the words, Danny knew how silly they sounded. Still, the more he thought about it, there was one clear person he should blame. It was his mum's fault. She had been the one to insist they moved house. If they had stayed where they were in London, his desk would have been against the wall in his old room. He wouldn't have had to dismantle it, move it 200 miles, rebuild it in a hurry and jam it under the window. Result: the vase would have been perfectly safe.

"Correction," Danny said with sudden confidence, "It was actually Mum's fault."

Ellie wasn't listening, she was still looking intently at the glued-up-vase. "This won't fool Mum."

Danny knew that glueing the vase would never be a permanent solution.

As soon as the glue had dried, they both took it downstairs. "Thanks for the help," Danny said, as he placed the vase back in its place near the window. It was far from perfect. Ellie was tugging carefully at the curtains.

"There, that's a bit better." She had pulled the edge of the curtain over the smaller window a little so the vase was in shadow.

"Unless she picks the vase up or gets really close," Danny said.

"Unless she comes into the room!" Ellie added.

Danny pulled a face. "I'll replace it as soon as I

can." Then, remembering he wanted to keep his sister sweet, he smiled brightly and added: "Do you have any money I can borrow?"

The question brought a sudden end to their temporary friendship.

"I think you know the answer to that," Ellie said. "I have some cash, but I'm buying Mum some perfume and any other money I'm saving." She stopped suddenly and smiled. Danny thought for a moment she was on the edge of changing her mind and offering to give him some money, the happy glimmer on her face had returned and the room seemed lighter somehow. "I want to get William a special gift at the end of the month."

Danny sighed, realising that the source of her happiness was the thought of her new 'friend' and not the result of any sisterly kindness. "Don't tell me it's his birthday too?"

"No," Ellie was still wearing a soppy look on her face. "On the 23rd it's our month-a-versary, we've known each other for—"

Danny didn't want to know. He needed to raise some cash, fast. He didn't have time for this, and he left the room while Ellie was in the middle of her sentence.

Spending any more time with her now would just be infuriating. In any case, he was beginning to think of an alternative way to get some extra money.

FOUR

A JOB TO DO

IN THE MOMENT that he left his sister with her warm thoughts of William, Danny instantly realised how he could raise the additional money. If his dad kept to his word, he would be able to replace the vase in no time. He imagined the delight on his mum's face on the morning of her birthday.

Danny went up to the bathroom, checked his face in the mirror. There were no cuts or bruises. Nothing hurt anymore. He found a graze on his left elbow, and this had marked his shirt. A quick change of clothing and everything looked fine once again. However, there was a dark bruise on the left side of his chest. He'd have to keep that covered for a few days. At least it didn't hurt.

He just had to make sure Ellie didn't tell anyone about his accident, and he would be in the clear. The good thing was, he already thinking of a way to keep her quiet. He would just have to sacrifice something he never used anyway.

With luck, his mum wouldn't notice any of his injuries, and there wouldn't be any awkward questions. Danny's mum was busy dashing around preparing things for her new school, she was the head teacher at Brendeg Primary. This new job, which was the main reason they had moved, was taking over her life. Danny knew better than to interrupt her.

He trotted downstairs to talk to his dad.

There was a grumbling noise from the dining room. That was his dad, struggling with some flat-pack furniture. Is this house never going to be finished? Back at his real home, all the rooms were perfect. Here, in this house, in this village, things were never quite right.

He missed his old home, the garden, his friends, the park. He even missed the neighbours, not that they'd ever been kind to him. But at least they were familiar.

Dad was busy trying to put together a cupboard, or was it a table? Danny wasn't sure what it was today.

He remembered that earlier in the week, his dad had offered him extra pocket money in return for help. That made him wonder about helping right now. He went to the door and looked into the narrow hall. His dad, Colin, was really a salesman and not a builder. He was struggling with a set of instructions and an enormous pile of chipboard, screws and plastic clips. It seemed to Danny that if building things was a competition, his dad was on the losing side. "Dad, can I help with that?"

His dad looked up from the box of furniture parts. He moved his big, awkward hands away from the two panels of wood he was holding together and adjusted his glasses. The panels immediately fell apart and collapsed back onto the floor. He cursed under his breath. "Normally, Danny, of course you could. But I need to get this done quickly."

"I can help quickly."

"Yes, I know." His dad was still adjusting his glasses. "But it is a bit awkward in here." He looked around the room. "With the other bits of furniture in here, there isn't enough space for two people to work on this at the same time." Picking up a pile of instructions, his dad waved them in the air. "And this seems to be written in Japanese."

Danny stepped closer, and made full use of his acting skills: "But, I want to help you."

That made his dad put the instructions down, the big man stood up and smiled. That was it, Danny thought. That smile was his signal.

"Dad, you said if I helped you would give me some extra pocket money?"

His dad's smile dropped away in a flash, "I seem to remember saying something like that."

"Well, do you have an idea of how much extra—"

"I guessed you would want to help just to be help-ful, son." He had had a look of disappointment on his face. Danny wondered if it was real disappointment, or if his dad too was working his acting muscles. He didn't have to wait long. "Danny, the money was an incentive, a kind of 'thank you'. You've annoyed me now. I think we should forget all about that particular bargain."

Then, as if it wasn't clear enough, he added: "I'm disappointed, Danny. Very disappointed." He turned back to the cupboard parts he'd been struggling to hold together, paused for a moment and then turned back. "Danny, you know what I've got packed up in a box upstairs?"

Danny knew. He didn't need to ask.

"I've still got my Les Paul Epiphone guitar, all carefully wrapped and stored in the bedroom." His dad paused dramatically, Danny waited. He wasn't sure where this part of the conversation was heading. Was there any money at the end of it?

"I'd love to unpack that guitar," he continued dreamily. "I'd love to stop struggling with this awkward cupboard and go up there and unpack it. Just to look at it. To run my hands over its faded cherry fretboard. You know?"

Danny didn't know, he wasn't even sure why it was important.

By now, his dad had put his tools down and was gripping an imaginary guitar. He looked up to the ceiling. "I'd love to play. Start a few riffs. Yeah." He strummed frantically on his fantasy guitar. Danny looked away. "I'd play really loud." He was half shouting above the imaginary guitar noise. "No neighbours here, you see. No one to demand I wear headphones. No one writing letters to the council. But do you know what?" He stopped abruptly, placed the invisible guitar on the floor and looked hard at his son.

Danny shook his head in the questioning pause his dad had left him.

His dad's face, which had held a happy smile when he spoke about his guitar, dropped back into a dark, brooding vision of disappointment. "I'm not going to do that, Danny. And do you know why I'm not going to do that?"

Danny could guess, but he let his dad finish.

"I'm not going to do it," his dad said, looking in frustration at the Japanese instructions again, "because I've got a job to do. And that comes first. Job first, reward later. Do you get it?"

Danny got it. He shrugged. So there wasn't any money at the end of this tale.

"Anyway, Danny," his dad's voice had a strangely suspicious tone. "Talking about money and rewards... Have you chosen a present for your mum yet?"

Danny gulped.

"I distinctly remember giving you extra money last week so you could buy her something nice. What have you been looking at?"

Danny gulped again.

FIVE
A PROFITABLE IDEA

His dad's question had surprised him. What could Danny say about this birthday present idea? He thought fast. "Oh, I'm still deciding. But I have a few plans." He hoped that would be enough information. He didn't want any more questions since his best birthday idea had just failed when that vase fell out of the window. Just to make his words sound more convincing, Danny added: "Don't worry, Dad. I've got it sorted." Of course, that was a small lie. But weren't people always saying that small lies can be good if they don't hurt anyone? This one certainly wasn't harmful, in fact, it acted as a double-sided protection. It saved his dad from worrying, and it saved him from being in trouble.

He stayed where he was, watching his dad as he struggled with the flat-pack cupboard. After a few minutes, Danny ended up passing tools or screws to him whenever he called for them. There wasn't much other conversation though, and Danny was happy about that.

Eventually, his dad broke the silence: "You could help your mum if you wanted. I think she's up in the office."

Danny shrugged, he didn't like that idea.

"No, wait," his dad continued. "I thought you promised your mum yesterday that you would sort out the bookcase in the living room?"

Yes, Danny remembered his promise. "Okay, I'll do it now." He felt he would be safer in a different room. He needed to think some more: 'Job first, money later'. Well, Danny was quite happy with that idea, provided the job part was quick, and the money part was large.

He headed into the living room. There were two bookcases in here. One was a huge monster of a thing, it sat squat and overloaded opposite the window. The other was a much smaller and slimmer, with around a dozen novels dotted on it. He'd promised to tidy a bookcase, but no one had made it clear which one! The decision was easy.

A moment later, a book moved here, and an ornament turned around there, and the tall, narrow bookcase looked magnificent. Danny stood back and marvelled at his handiwork.

There was one part that didn't quite look right, though. A scruffy looking box spoilt the bottom shelf. Danny knew with total certainty that if his mum saw the bookcase, she would ignore all of the remarkably well-organised shelves and only notice the untidy box at the bottom. He swiftly pulled the box out and hunted through it. A quick sort and he'd put it back. What was this anyway? Why were there so many odd leaflets and advertisements here?

Lots of the papers were totally out of date. A leaflet advertising a river cruise was for the year before. Another one about a train ride was still okay, but he noticed the voucher on the back had run out in December. Most of the things in the box would have to go to recycling; they were so old and tatty no one would ever want to read them.

There was a brightly coloured newsletter advertising a Shakespeare picnic in the park event, whatever that was. A dull looking advert for a boat trip in a disused mine caught his eye. That could be interesting, but why was it here?

The next bit of paper gave him the biggest clue. It explained the opening hours for the county library. One side was in English and the other side in Welsh. Of course, these were one of his mum's bright ideas. The first week they moved to Brendeg she had decided to get a selection of these 'What's on Guide's' from the library. Here they were, totally unused and unread, and tucked inside this shabby box. He knew what to do: Lose the box and stack the leaflets back on the shelf between two fat books. That would make all the shelves look equally tidy and smart. Mum would be impressed.

The box went in a black bin bag, and he was rapidly sliding the leaflets on a shelf when something made him stop and look again. The leaflet in his hand was a simple home-made A5 poster. Blue ink on white. But it wasn't the style or printing that made him think, it was the words:

CAR BOOT SALE
Grindley Fields
Saturday, March 10th

LIKE MOST OF the other advertisements, it was totally out of date. What did they do in the library, store these things up for years?

Never mind the date, though. There was an idea here.

Danny stared at the text again, thinking.

In a moment, he had made a major decision.

He quickly picked up all the remaining papers and jammed them on the shelf wherever there was a space. It didn't matter anymore. He'd had an idea. An idea that was going to be fun and profitable.

COLIN LOOKED up as the living room door opened, and his son rushed out.

"You're doing great, Dad," he heard Danny say as he charged past and headed upstairs.

Colin thought about stopping him and trying to explain again about the pocket money. *Maybe I was a little hard on him earlier.* He thought as he struggled with an odd hinge-fixing on the cupboard door. *Perhaps I should have gone ahead with giving him a reward of some kind.*

He knew Danny was upset about something.

A clamour of loud footsteps thundered overhead, and Colin looked up at the newly painted ceiling, fretting about the treatment the plaster was receiving from above.

He wondered for a moment if it was the house move that had upset Danny. But no, everyone had been happy to leave stuffy London behind and move to this lovely town. It can't be that, but perhaps... Colin nodded quietly to himself, he guessed his son was worried about starting at a new school. New house, new school, new friends. It was a lot for him to cope with. He looked at the instructions for the hundredth time, making a mental note to talk this over with Danny later in the day.

The hinge in Colin's hands slipped out of its place and the door tilted forwards again. He stamped his hand down on the unreadable instructions.

There was too much to do.

SIX

THE PRICE OF MY SILENCE

Upstairs in his bedroom once more, Danny surveyed the boxes. The best games, toys and books had already been unpacked. He looked around at the temporary shelving. All of his most valuable possessions were there, not tidy, but at least unpacked. What remained, in five large cardboard boxes were all the things that he had kept, just in case. Well, he gritted his teeth in determination. This was the moment they had been waiting for. He could put them to good use now.

Without even looking inside any of the boxes, he piled them up by his bedroom door, making quite a bit of noise in the process. Then, he dragged them one by one downstairs and into the front yard.

On the third trip, he met Ellie in the hallway. She seemed especially pleased with herself.

She looked at his clean clothes. "You look better."

"Thanks, you won't tell anyone what happened, will you?"

She smiled sweetly. "Probably not."

"Well, I'd like to make that 'certainly not'"

Ellie looked interested, she gestured for him to continue.

Now it was Danny's turn to smile. "You know you wanted to borrow my selfie stick the other day?"

"Yes, you were awful about it."

"Well, I'm sorry. More than that, I've decided that you can borrow it." Danny waited for her to look happy, and then said: "In fact, you can keep it."

"The price of my silence?"

"Of course. Oh, there is one condition, though."

"Yes?"

"I absolutely never, ever, ever want to see any of the photos you take with it."

"Ha, Ha," Ellie said and waved him away with her hand. "That's a deal. I do love you, little brother."

Danny pulled a face and pretended to be sick.

Ellie ignored him. "You'll also be pleased to know that I've sent William a text. He's going to get his brother to come over to play with you." She gave him her brightest smile.

William and his brother lived with their family a few houses away in Hollowford Road. Danny had never met them, but within the first hours of moving house, his sister had. They were going to be in the same form in high school. Danny would be with Luke, but that didn't mean he wanted to meet him.

"You only want me to be friends with Luke so you can see William."

"Don't be silly. I don't have any interest in William," Ellie said. Then she paused and bit her lip.

"Oh no…" Danny said, watching her eyes go all misty.

Ellie started tapping on her phone.

"What are you doing?"

Ellie was distracted. She didn't look up. "Just sorting something out for you."

Danny shrugged. He didn't need a new friend. If he was on his own here, it was because they had moved hundreds of miles away from his old friends. He thought his life was a bit like the vase - fractured and out of place. And no, he glared at Ellie, some little Luke kid was not going to be the glue to him back together. It felt like things were closing in on him. Looking over the garden wall, he could see fields and green hills for miles. Why, if they now lived in such a wide open-place, did he feel so trapped?

Danny shrugged and returned to dragging the boxes out of the house. "I don't know this Luke kid," he called over his shoulder.

Halfway to the gate, he stopped: "I don't like him…"

When he got to the gate: "I don't want to like him…"

He picked the box up and banged it back down on the floor noisily: "I don't want to meet him."

Finally, he paused for extra emphasis before raising his voice to say: "Ever!"

Behind him, Ellie was heading back inside. She glanced at her phone. "He's coming over," she said.

There was a faint hope that Ellie meant William was coming. Danny could cope with William. He could ignore him and not get into trouble. But if she had meant 'Luke is coming' that would be more of a problem.

He kicked the bottom step. Of course, it wouldn't be a problem if Luke had loads of money and wanted to give him some. Yes, Luke might be so desperate he would want to buy his friendship. About £45 should do it!

Excited by this encouraging, but not totally serious thought, Danny went hunting in the garage. After a house move, it was amazing what you could find. Some things that no one ever used were now within easy reach. He quickly found and pulled out the old wallpaper pasting table. He set it up at the edge of the front yard, close to the pavement so that it could not be missed by anyone walking past.

Two boxes were opened, and without a second thought, he arranged the old games, books and toys on the table.

Back upstairs to the spare bedroom, which was now

acting as an office. He looked in at his mum. She was sifting through some school papers.

"Sorry Mum, can I just borrow——"

His mum, Helen, looked up from the desk. "Oh Danny, can you wait just a minute? Let me think." His mum pulled open a file box while Danny watched, then she carefully counted out a handful of papers into it, closed the box, checked her phone and stood up.

"Sorry, Danny. I have to pop out for a couple of hours. What was it you wanted, love?"

Danny explained as quickly as he could, picking up the felt pens and papers he had come to collect.

"Are you playing nicely?" his mum asked. "No tricks? Remember, we are new around here and want to give people a good impression. Right?"

Danny nodded and raced back downstairs. He wrote 'FOR SALE' on the paper in large capital letters and taped it to the front edge of the table.

The whole process, from idea to sorting the toys and setting up the table, had taken less than 20 minutes. You didn't need to go to a proper car boot sale to sell things. This was fine.

Danny rubbed his hands together like a shopkeeper and leaned over his table of goods to wait for his first customer.

SEVEN
ARE THESE FOR SALE?

EVERYTHING WAS PERFECTLY ARRANGED. Anyone passing the house would immediately see the wonderful array of goods. Naturally, they would then all dash in to buy something.

There was a faint noise coming from beyond the gate, Danny leant over the table and saw a cat walk past. No sale.

He thought the cat had gone, but it suddenly jumped onto the low wall beside the gate and purred at him. Danny looked at it carefully. He'd seen it around the yard before, a dirty looking black and white thing. He knew some people who would 'Ooh...' and 'Ahh...' over it, but it just looked fat and ugly to him. He guessed it smelled too.

He picked up an old Christmas album and waved it angrily until the cat dashed away.

The road was quiet and empty now.

Danny waited a few minutes. No customers appeared. He looked up and down the road, sighed loudly, adjusted the contents of the table and sighed again. This was getting boring. He needed to sit down.

Danny wondered about getting a chair from the kitchen. He guessed this sort of thing would take time, and he wasn't going to stand up for the rest of the day.

"Is this your slipper?" The words cut across his need to sit.

Danny peered over the assorted games and books to see a small boy with pale brown hair and a perfectly round face. He looked a little like a cartoon of a boy, and if he had been wearing bright blue or bright red, he could easily have sneaked into an episode of The Simpsons and not been out of place.

The boy was holding a red and white striped slipper. Danny immediately recognised it.

"Yes, that's mine. Thank you." Danny took the slipper and casually threw it in a box behind him.

"It was in the street," the boy told him. Then, looking at the collection of things on the table added: "Are these for sale?"

Danny had a split second to decide how to answer the question. It was a stupid question since the answer was written in large capital letters (and in red ink) on the paper directly in front of the table. But, if the boy had money, Danny needed to be polite. This could be his first sale. However, if this strange little comedy-boy didn't have money, he should go away and fast.

Danny stared at him, "Are these for sale?" he repeated the question slowly, keeping his face expressionless until he had made his judgement. "Yes," he smiled broadly and waved his arm to indicate everything on the table. "The whole lot is for sale, what would you like?" He'd decided the boy was worth the test... He could be loaded.

"Oh, I don't want anything," the boy replied. His voice was a little squeaky, and since he was not going to buy anything, Danny decided it wasn't just a squeaky voice, but a horribly squeaky voice. "I've come to help you."

At that, Danny's heart sank again. The 'I'm not going to buy anything' was a huge blow. The words 'I'm here to help you' was like a firm kick in the ribs. He imagined the pain would hit him right where his new bruise was. By now, Danny had worked it out. "You're Luke Ellis?" he said.

"Yep, I certainly am," the boy squeaked, although the tone of his voice was more confident. "...And I guess you're Danny." At that, the squeaky-boy, or Luke, as Danny was forced to think of him from now on, stretched out his hand as if he wanted it to be shaken.

Danny was too shaken himself to shake anyone else. This was maddening, he was sure his sister had done this deliberately to annoy him.

The more he thought about, it the more concerned he became. The real issue was that this odd little boy had been able to come charging across town to be with him at a moment's notice. What did that tell you? It made it abundantly clear that Luke had nothing to do, and no friends to do it with. In school, Luke was probably the class nerd. And although Danny didn't have any friends in town yet, he certainly didn't want to start with his first friend being this Luke character.

"Well, I'm a bit busy…"

"I'd like to help," Luke said with a smile. Then he looked again at the table of toys and games. "I like this," he picked up one of Danny's old medals. It was a WWII war medal, not one from his grandad or anyone he knew. In fact, Danny couldn't remember where it had come from.

Luke put the medal back down again, "If I had my money with me I would buy that one. How much is it?"

Danny liked that question. Maybe Luke wasn't as bad as he first seemed. "£5," Danny said without hesitation. He had no idea how much it was worth, it seems like a common medal, he remembered looking it up on the internet a few years ago when he first found it.

"Expensive!" said Luke.

"Very rare," said Danny.

"Then why are you selling it?"

"I need…" Danny said, then thought carefully before adding: "…to make more room in my bedroom."

"This tiny thing won't make you that much room," Luke said.

Luke was looking around him. He looked like a

Labrador dog sniffing out food. Then he pointed up to the house behind Danny. "Is it nice?"

"I suppose it is. We're redecorating. We've only been here a week. There's lots to do."

"Have you seen the ghost?"

"What?" Danny was confused.

"Someone told me this old house was haunted."

"It's one of the oldest houses in town. The estate agent told my mum it had been empty for a while." Danny said. "But the only bad thing in there is the smell of damp."

Luke was looking around again. "Where are the trees?"

Danny stared. In the past, people had told him he didn't focus, that his mind jumped from one thing to another. He remembered his mum calling it 'Butterfly brain', his dad had a ruder name for it. But whatever it was, this limited concentration thing that caused him to flit from idea to idea… Well, it seemed that Luke suffered from it too. All Danny could do in response to the question about the trees was stare. He had no words.

"The oak trees…" Luke was still talking. "You don't have any oak trees." With that, he waved his arm around to take in the surroundings. There was the old ivy-covered house; the gravel drive; the low stone wall; the roadway behind them and grassy banks to the left and right. No trees.

The arm waving demonstration gave Danny a

moment to understand Luke's thoughts. It was the house's name.

"Ah, yes," Danny said. "The house is called 'The Oaks'. I've no idea why, though. The estate agent said—"

Luke seemed to have lost interest, he was picking up Danny's things one at a time. He held up an old wooden bookend with a horse's head carved into it. "My mum would buy this. She loves horses."

"You can have it for £5." Danny didn't really like the bookend, "No, since it's for your mum, you can buy it for £4. It's a bargain."

"Nah, I can't afford it."

"£3 then."

Luke shook his head.

"Don't you have any money?"

Luke shook his head again.

Danny smiled. "Join the club."

EIGHT

A BAD INFLUENCE

LUKE HAD TURNED his attention back to the WWII medal. "My dad has a metal detector. If we searched I bet we could find more of these in the fields."

Danny was busy looking over his shoulder. Some other people were walking up the road. A couple turned off early, so those customers were lost. But then, a thin man who looked like he could be a gamekeeper stopped next to the gate.

"This is nice," the man said, but he didn't seem to be talking about any specific thing, but looking at the whole table. Did he want to buy the table, Danny wondered. "This is a good idea." the man said, nodding to himself.

What a nice, kind looking man. Danny could see he was heading for a sale here and smiled broadly.

The man smiled back. "Are you raising money for charity?"

"Well…" Danny heard himself say. Then he was surprised to find he had also added the words: "Yes, of course!" He was conscious that Luke was standing right next to him, listening. If he'd been alone, he might have made the charity story a little more interesting, and the man would probably have bought something. Especially if he was selling things for an old person's charity, or medical research, or to send his sick brother to hospital… anything. That's what George would have done. His old school friend was always happy to tell anybody anything if it resulted in a profit. Danny was a little less certain. He hopped awkwardly from foot to foot.

"Are you alright?" the man wanted to know.

This was awkward. His mum used to say, 'That George will lead you into trouble.' Well, maybe George did, once or twice (or maybe three times). But that was the past. That was George. He, Danny James didn't want Luke's mum pointing an angry finger and saying, 'That Danny is a bad influence on you, Luke…'

Danny's plastic smile was only skin deep. He looked down at the items on the table, but his mind was still on the man in front of him as he tried to will him to forget the details. Please don't ask me which charity. I can lie a little, but naming a specific charity would feel bad.

It was quiet for a moment and when Danny built up the courage to look up again, the old man was walking away. "There's a fun run next weekend," the man said over his shoulder. "You should enter that, they are raising money for the RSPCA."

"Thank you," Danny called after him. But he didn't feel a thank you was that much deserved.

When he turned his gaze back to Luke, he found the younger boy staring at him with a peculiar look on his face. "You should have told him you were collecting for an injured puppy or something. He would have liked that…"

Danny, his mouth gaping, just stared.

Luke ignored the stare and continued explaining. "That was Mr Jonas, his son is the Caretaker at the Secondary School. They have loads and loads of dogs. Little snappy things, my mum says. The whole family is animal crazy." Luke paused briefly to take in a lungful of fresh air. Then rushed on with more information. "Dogs, cats, rabbits and donkeys. They've got the lot. Now, if you'd said you were collecting for an animal charity, he would have bought most of this stuff." He paused for a moment to look at the collection of things on the table. "Yes, he'd buy any old rubbish for a good cause."

Danny didn't like the way he'd said, 'rubbish' but then Luke added a few words that he did like.

"You see," Luke was saying. "You have to know these people, once you know them you will know how to get around them…"

At that moment Danny realised he didn't need to worry about 'leading Luke astray'. He was in the presence of a boy as sneaky and cunning as George. He'd been trying to protect this Luke from bad deeds, and here he was positively spilling over with cheats and scams of his own. Danny was also surprised to find that during the conversation, he had walked around the table to be on the same side as Luke.

In the brief pause during which Danny was thinking hard, and Luke seemed to be counting clouds, there was only silence. Then a voice broke in.

"Danny, what are you doing?"

He turned to see his mum. He started to explain about the table sale, but Helen had already noticed.

"Oh, that's a lovely idea," she said with a smile that shocked Danny. Then, looking at Luke, she added: "And I recognise your friend, don't I? Are you William's brother?"

Luke said he was. Danny noticed that the poor lad was almost standing to attention. He smiled to himself. His mum often had that effect on people.

"Lovely to meet you." Danny's mum then turned this brand new smile towards him. "Danny, it's good to see you sorting out your things. Let's hope you can make plenty of space in your room. Have you sold much?"

Danny started to answer, but his mum wasn't listening. She charged on with more questions. "Would you like a drink? Orange juice? Lemonade perhaps? It's great to see you two playing together. Have you eaten? Would you like a biscuit?"

They sorted out drinks and biscuits, then Helen hurried back inside.

"Your mum is nice," Luke said.

Danny didn't reply, his mind was on other things. That had been an amazing moment. He hadn't sold a thing, but his mum had seen him doing something she felt was a 'good thing', and that was always useful. She had seemed genuinely pleased. Danny gave a small 'Hurray' and clinked his glass with Luke. If Luke was puzzled by this, he didn't show it. It seemed to Danny that Luke was so desperate for a friend he would accept anything. Isn't that basically what Ellie had said?

All of this cheer wouldn't pay the bills though, and Danny could not get away from the real problem: He still needed a way to find £45.

NINE

EVERYTHING WILL WORK OUT FINE

Two more hours passed, Luke had come round to the back of the table to help. A woman with a pushchair had looked as she strolled past, a girl with a skipping rope had stopped to ask if they had any chewing gum. A man had waited for a moment with his Jack Russell. The man had glanced at the books, and his dog left a damp patch at the bottom of one of the table legs. But no one bought anything.

It took Luke to point out the obvious: "I don't think you're going to sell anything." He looked thoughtful and then added, "You're doing this on the wrong day, of course. It would be better to sell things at the weekend, especially Sunday. We always get lots of visitors to the town on a Sunday; they love to come to walk in the hills or explore. We get loads of tourists at the weekend."

Danny had to agree. "This is far too slow. I can't

wait until the weekend. I need to think of another way to raise money," he said.

"You told me you wanted to make more space in your bedroom."

"Ah," Danny squirmed a little. He'd said too much already, but he decided to say even more. "Yes, that's partly right… but there's more to it than that." He felt that even though he didn't particularly like Luke, he could probably trust him, so he decided to tell him the whole story.

"Well if you need £45, this is a pretty poor way of going about it." Luke's words were harsh, but Danny knew there was sense in them.

"I've been trying to think of a better way…"

"Is there anything else you can sell?"

"No."

"Can you offer to do something…?"

"Like what?"

Luke's face seemed to squirm, and Danny decided that this is what he did when he was deep in thought. Then, after a few moments of face-jiggling Luke grinned. "We could wash cars."

Danny shrugged. All that effort for such a lame suggestion. "It's a thought," Danny said. It was the only kind reply he could offer. "Where I used to live, that would be a great idea. We could charge £2 a shot and earn the money in a couple of afternoons. In Hanwell, there were loads of people with cars and spare money." He waved his arms around to indicate the empty street.

"Here, I've only seen three cars on this entire road. Do you think we could find 20 people willing to let us wash their car?"

"We could charge more."

"The garage wash down the road only charges £2."

The two boys fell silent as they each tried to figure out a different way to get the money.

LUKE WAS GETTING BORED.

He had watched Danny rearrange the items on the table dozens of times. No one had bought anything, and no matter how hard he tried, he could not find any of this enjoyable. He had a better idea but wondered if Danny would even listen to him. It seemed that Danny could be quite bossy.

"I've been thinking," Luke finally decided it was worth testing his idea. "I've got a better way to raise money than washing cars. My dad's astronomy club just had a raffle and—"

Danny was putting all the CD's in a pile in front of the paperback books. "Astronomy club? I thought you said your dad had a metal detector?"

Luke nodded. "Yes, he does. He sometimes goes metal detecting at the weekend. He goes star-gazing in the winter. My dad has tons of hobbies. Sometimes he sticks to them for two or three whole weeks. Anyway..." Luke was certain Danny would interrupt again, so he paused. Danny seemed to be waiting patiently, so he continued: "Anyway, his club had a raffle, and they raised nearly £1000. My dad organised it all. It was great. Could we have a raffle? What about that?"

Luke knew the raffle idea was a certain winner, and he waited eagerly for Danny to show how excited he was. There was silence, and Luke found himself staring at his own shoes. It reminded him of the times he had suggested good stories in English lessons, neither the teacher nor anyone else in class ever seemed to like his ideas.

"I've done a raffle before," Danny shook his head as he moved the paperback books to the back of the table. "It didn't turn out well. A schoolmate persuaded me to raffle our next-door neighbour's dog. Not a good idea." There was a long pause while Danny looked sad and Luke watched him. Then Danny added quietly. "It's not worth doing. Far too much hassle."

Luke picked up the books and placed them back at the front of the table.

"Wait a minute," Danny made him jump. "That metal detector you mentioned. Do you think we could borrow it?"

Luke nodded energetically. The dull calm quiet of the afternoon had suddenly changed. "Ooh, yes," he said, pleased that something he'd suggested was useful. "We could search the grounds of the school for treasure."

Danny pulled a face, and Luke felt a little embarrassed. "I'm not thinking about pirates' treasure." Luke needed to correct any babyish images Danny might have been creating. "I mean lost jewellery," he said. "You know, old medals or coins."

Danny stared at him, and Luke thought he spotted a strange glint in his eyes. "This metal detector," Danny said slowly. "Can you get it tomorrow?"

Luke nodded. "Dad hasn't used it for months."

"Right." There was a sharp business-like sense to Danny's voice. "My dad will be shouting me in for dinner soon. Let's tidy all this away. Can you bring the metal detector first thing in the morning?"

Luke was sure he could and said so. Then he helped Danny to empty the table and tidy away the boxes. Chiefly, this meant throwing all of Danny's games and toys into the boxes and stacking them up in the entrance hall. The boxes, even piled one on top of the other, took up a lot of room. Luke knew that if he had done this at his house, he would instantly be in trouble. Danny seemed to be unconcerned, however. Following Danny's advice, he managed to wedge the boxes in the corner behind the coat stand. A quick tug at some of the thicker coats and everything was hidden.

"I'm not lugging them back upstairs," Danny explained. "We might need them out here again in a couple of days."

Just as he was leaving Luke had another thought. He was quite pleased with this one. "Danny, since we are using my metal detector—"

"Your dad's metal detector." Danny corrected him as he led him outside.

"Yes. But what I mean is, we really ought to share everything we find."

"Of course."

"Fifty-fifty?"

Danny didn't reply immediately, but Luke found the gate had been opened for him and he was being waved on his way. "I'm sure everything will work out fine," Danny said.

That cheered Luke up, and he raced off home. He was looking forward to tomorrow.

TEN

THE XP-5 METAL HUNTER

THE NEXT MORNING AFTER BREAKFAST, Danny waited for his dad to go into the dining room to continue building furniture. His mum had gone up to her office-junk-room to sort through papers. Ellie had said she was going into town to do some shopping.

With everyone busy, it was easy for Danny to disappear. He pulled out his old school rucksack, dropped in a couple of drinks and biscuits and met Luke at the gate. He had considered waiting in the house for him but just knew that his mum and dad would spot him and make a fuss, and that would make it seem Danny was friendless. While he did miss some of his old mates, he certainly didn't need a new special friend. It made him feel babyish again. He still missed George. With George, he found they could start a conversation and carry it on several days later. Good friends always knew what each other was thinking.

He stood at the gate and looked down the road. He'd been waiting for a few minutes now, and his mind was wondering. He stood on the gate, swinging it on its rusty creaking hinges. He leaned over the gate, holding on with his hands as he tipped his body forwards, almost like a trapeze artist. He swung out again, the gate creaked.

He was searching down the road when he heard the door slam behind him. His sister was standing directly behind him.

"Oh," she said when she saw that she couldn't get through the gate. "Are you waiting for your friend Luke?"

Danny pulled a face.

"Don't worry," She said as she pushed past him. "I think it's great that you are playing with him."

"I'm not five... we're not **playing**." Danny looked at her and decided to tell her what he was planning.

She was still walking away while he explained. For a moment, he thought she wasn't listening, but then she turned around and said: "But, why?"

Danny frowned, jumped off the gate and looked at her carefully as though he wasn't sure if she was well or not. "Your memory is about as good as Dad's," he said. "I need the money for the vase... remember?"

His sister nodded, "I know, I remember. I'm not the idiot. But I thought you had sorted all that out. Mum said you were selling some of your old things. I guessed that was your way of making money for the vase. You sold everything, didn't you?"

"I didn't sell anything! There's no one here to buy anything." He waved his arms around to emphasise how empty the place was. He wanted to add, 'this isn't London, you know.' But he was stopped by the arrival of Luke.

His new friend - ugh he hated that word - appeared from around the corner, carrying a large black plastic bag. The bag was old, tatty and looked like something Luke had found buried in a skip.

Danny didn't want to ask because he felt he already knew the answer, but the state of the bag meant he just had to say: "What's that?"

Luke pulled the bag from over his shoulder and plumped it down on the floor. There was some long thin object in the bag, and it could have been a rifle by the shape of it.

"This is the XP-5 Metal Hunter," Luke explained as he pulled the crumpled black plastic away from the metal detector. "There's an XP-6 out now, which can detect different metals 10cm deep in the ground. But this one is just fine." He said as he rubbed his hands lovingly over the machine. It looked like a black and silver spade handle had been fastened onto a flat grey circular disk. Luke held it up. He flicked a switch, and the detector emitted a low hum.

Luke waved the device around in the air until the circular detection plate came close to Ellie's belt. The machine gave out a piercing screech until Luke moved it away again.

"Congratulations..." Ellie said, "You found my belt." Then she turned to walk away. "Good luck boys."

Luke handed the machine to Danny and started explaining what the buttons were for. Behind them, the door banged again, and the gate creaked. Danny's mum shot through the gate and past them. "Have fun," she called out as she sped past. "Got to go into school this afternoon." She paused to turn back. "Danny, your dad will sort out your tea, be back in before six. Ok?" She didn't wait for a reply, but turned away again, calling out as she ran down the road, "Be careful. Don't take that machine into people's gardens. See you later. Bye."

"Is the primary school open today?" Luke asked as they wrapped the detector back up in the bag.

"No, it's not open until September. But she's the new head teacher. She's always planning, texting, preparing or sorting some important things out." Danny explained while he was busy studying the metal detector. "Your dad's okay with us using this?" he said again, the whole thing looked expensive.

"Er, yes," Luke said, but there was a faint hesitation in his voice. Danny was a long-time expert at inventing excuses and hearing other people make up stories. He recognised the hesitation in Luke's voice.

"Are you 'borrowing' it?" Danny watched Luke's face. "Or does he know you have it?"

"He won't mind," Luke said. To Danny, this was a clear admission. But Danny quite liked that, it seemed to show him again that Luke had some spirit.

In some ways, Danny was yet to be convinced of the value of this little plan. He'd fallen into using the metal detector partially because it sounded like a good idea, but he knew that the realities were that they would have to be lucky to find anything of any real value.

"Come on," Luke said, "I know just where to go with this. There's a field behind the old post office where they once found some Victorian coins. There's a good chance there'll be something there."

Danny looked up, that was better, his luck may be changing.

"If we do find something though," he said, as they walked. "We'll have to think of a way to turn it into proper money. I can't buy a vase with a couple of ancient coins, can I?"

"Let's just see what we find."

They walked along Fosse Lane. The Post Office had clearly been a house in the past, it was at the end of a short row of terraced houses. Each with a small yard to the rear.

Luke stopped and then pointed up a narrow gap between the post office and the garage next door. "Through here." He set off, the Metal-Hunter rocking on his shoulder as he jogged up the slight slope between the buildings.

A cat cried out loudly as they passed and darted into an open window.

At the top of the passage, the buildings opened out onto a field. Luke took a path that ran behind the row of houses and out towards a large sloping field. A low wall ran round it, and the edge was dotted with old trees and in a few places some thick bushes. The two boys walked up to the wall, and Danny noticed that part of it was crumbled away. Luke made for this part, and they clambered over.

"No one uses this field now. A farmer used to have sheep in here, but he's not done that for months. We are okay here."

As soon as he said this, a gruff voice called at them from behind. They turned to see a large man framed in the narrow slit of the alleyway.

"Hello," Luke called cheerfully, and he waved.

"Where are you two off to?" The man called out. Danny noticed he had a small dog with him.

"Just exploring, Mr Jackson," Luke called back. He swung the Metal-Hunter machine to one side, and Danny suddenly realised that it probably looked like a shotgun from a distance.

Luke unwrapped the detector and folded the bag up and held it under his arm. He turned the machine on and showed Danny how to hold the handle and wave the detection plate over the ground.

Danny immediately took over, but he was careful to work the machine properly. The first few waves of the detector produced nothing. He waved it around in a wide arc. Still nothing.

Then, a moment later, the device gave out a loud whine.

Danny grinned.

Luke sighed. "That's probably a ring pull or a metal cap. People often walk here, there's a lot of bits of rubbish." He took the detector from Danny and started walking up the field with it. "We may have better luck further up, away from the houses."

Mr Jackson was watching from a distance.

"Hold on," Danny said. "Let's just stay here for a few more minutes."

"But he's watching us."

"I know."

The boys took it in turns to operate the metal detector, sweeping in gentle arcs across the ground. Once or twice the detector let out a loud peeping noise as though it had discovered something. Danny noticed that Mr Jackson seemed to look at them with much more interest whenever this happened. However, whenever Danny looked across to him, the man was staring at the ground, talking to his dog.

"Let's have some fun," Danny said and took control of the metal detector.

ELEVEN
GOOD PICKINGS ON THESE HILLS

WITH MR JACKSON and his dog watching from some distance away, Danny and Luke continued using the metal detector. Luke thought they were looking for treasure. Danny was working on a little plan of his own. He waved the circular plate at the foot of the machine gently over the ground and secretly pressed the 'test' button. The detector beeped.

Danny increased the volume. Moved the sensor plate a little over the grass and pressed the 'test' button again. The beep was loud, and he held the button for a long time just to be sure Mr Jackson had heard.

Continuing with the pretence, Danny looked carefully at the ground. He bent and picked something up. His hand was empty, but he mimed holding a small object. He showed it to Luke.

Luke looked at Danny's empty hand and then at Danny. "What are you doing?" he asked.

"Shh. Quiet."

Luke tried again, this time in a whisper: "What are you doing?"

"I told you. I'm just having a bit of fun." Out of the corner of his eye, he noticed Mr Jackson was looking in their direction. He was walking his dog up and down the same patch of grass many more times than necessary. It was clear that he was fascinated by what they were doing.

Danny swung his rucksack off of his back and put his hand inside, pretending to place something precious he had just found carefully inside.

As he replaced the rucksack the man called out to them, "Are you having any luck?"

"Just a little," Danny said, which wasn't true unless you counted it lucky to find grass and sheep droppings in a grassy sheep field.

"There's good pickings on these hills." The man replied.

That made little sense to Danny. But he nodded eagerly. He decided to keep the story going a little. After all, he told himself, his old mate George would have loved this type of thing, "We've found about half a dozen... very interesting things."

"Oh?" the man shouted.

Luke suddenly seemed to get the idea and excitedly added: "Yes, some jewellery and medals."

"But mainly coins." Danny interrupted, digging his elbow into Luke's stomach. Then he lowered his voice to hiss at his friend, "Keep it realistic. We're hardly going to find jewellery are we?" He paused. "I've got an idea. Let him think we have some coins here."

The man stopped pacing and looked intently at them. "Oh, do you mind if I take a look?" He started heading towards them.

Danny realised this was a dead end. If he carried on, he'd be caught in the lie. "We'll look a little further along." He called out and started to move along the bank towards the top of the hill. "We'll come back and show you. We may find even more."

"Oh, okay. I'll be inside." The man waved toward the post office. "Young Luke there knows me. Okay?"

"Yes, Mr Jackson," Luke said quietly.

The two boys waved.

"Call me Albert," Mr Jackson said, walking away slowly. "Don't forget now. I'll be in there all day."

The boys raced up the hill, trying not to laugh.

"Why did you do that?" Luke asked. "We'll have to find something to show him now."

"Nah, don't worry about it. He'll forget. Adults always do." Danny started packing the machine away. "Come on, we ought to go. When he comes out of the post office, he might try to find us again."

"He won't come out."

"What?"

"He owns it. I see him every day. He's a horrible man. He's well known around here for giving people the wrong change. Once he gave William change for a

£5 note when he'd paid with a £10. Old Mr Jackson won't forget. Can't we tell him we were mistaken?"

"We could, I suppose." Then Danny stopped. He was thinking again. "Do you suppose Mr Jackson would like to buy some old coins?"

Luke stared at him, "What? Even if he did, we don't have any."

Danny shrugged and said, "I do. I have some Roman coins back in those boxes. Didn't you see them?" Then he paused for a moment while he worked on the idea a little more. "We bought them at a museum a few years ago." He remembered how excited he had been at the time to open up the little plastic pocket and feel the old coins. They weren't valuable, of course, but they looked the part. "We can sell him those."

"Will he believe they're worth anything?"

"He will if they're covered in dirt, and he thinks we dug them out of this field." By now Danny had convinced himself the idea was a good one. No, it was a great idea. The kind of idea George might have suggested. The trick would work, but the key, he realised, was in making everyone believe the coins came out of the ground. "Let's get back to my house. I'll get the coins, we need to start making them look really dirty."

Before Luke could argue or offer an alternative suggestion, Danny had set off at a pace. He left the metal detector lying on the ground.

Luke had no other option than to chase after him. He picked up the metal detector, swung it over his shoulder, and raced off.

"Can we stop all this racing about now?" Luke said, "I'm out of breath here." They had arrived back at The Oaks.

Danny gave no reply. It was as though he wasn't interested.

Luke leant the metal detector against the wall and rubbed the back of his leg. "I think I've trapped a nerve."

Danny was waiting by the gate. "Come on. I have this ingenious plan to raise some cash, and all you can do is moan."

TWELVE

AT THE BOTTOM OF THE LAST BOX

THAT EVENING DANNY scrabbled in the hallway for the boxes from his bedroom. He pulled them out from their hiding place and started to hunt through them.

"Danny, you need to be here for your dinner." His mum called from the kitchen.

Normally, Danny would have moaned about the idea of eating at the table in the kitchen, he preferred sitting in front of the TV, usually with a plate of ham sandwiches. Most evening though the family had this ritual of sitting at the table with food on plates and knives and forks and everything. Danny hated it. Right now though, he was too busy searching in the boxes to have time to be unhappy about that. "I'm on my way…" he shouted, pulling out all the things he and Luke had put away the previous day: jigsaws, pens, pencils, woollen hats, horse bookends, a plastic Yo-Yo won at a fair and an ancient alarm clock he had used since he was six. Everything spilt out of the boxes.

Why was it that the one thing he wanted would be at the bottom of the last box?

"Danny?" that was his mum again.

"I'm coming right now." Danny remained where he was, surrounded by bits of things he had collected or found over the past half-dozen years. Ah, here was his old pet rock. It was a large pebble from the beach with eyes drawn on with a marker pen. He'd forgotten about this. It was called Eric, and it used to sit on his window ledge.

Something pulled at his sleeve, and he looked up.

Ellie had her face close to his, and through gritted teeth, she said: "Your dinner's on the table. It's getting cold and Mum's getting cross."

Oh. Danny dropped the pebble back into the box. He stood up and headed into the kitchen. Just as he closed the door, something caught his eye. Sticking out from beneath the box was a small packet. He knew what it was, a slim re-sealable bag which held five replica Roman coins.

"That's it…" he wanted to head back and grab it, but he knew it would be safe for a while, and dinner was on the table.

Dinner was Cheesy pasta. Probably his favourite, but tonight it tasted like damp cardboard. His mind was on other things.

Ellie and his dad were busy chatting together.

Although it wasn't quite a conversation. Ellie was talking about some silly video she had seen on Facebook. His mum was asking if Ellie was all ready for her new class. If he had been listening properly, Danny would have found it funny.

Dad threw in a question: "And do you have everything you need?"

Danny was thinking that if he took the coins out of the plastic bag and mixed them with some mud, he could make them look even older and more realistic. He had a tub in his bedroom, he could put some soil in that.

Mum's voice: "Your pencil case, have you made sure it has new pens in? There's only a few more days until school starts."

Soil in the tub, bury the coins overnight and rub the dirt in really hard. Maybe try to grind it in somehow. Or, what if he warmed the coins up? Could he put them in the microwave—?

"Danny!"

The room came into focus, and he realised Ellie, his mum and his dad were all staring at him.

"I've been asking you for five minutes about your school bag and your pencil case." His mum said. Ah, that explained her angry expression.

"Oh."

"You've been sitting there, ignoring me."

"I thought you were talking to Ellie."

"Half asleep." His mum stamped the words out. "What day is it?"

"Er?" Danny was confused. Was this some kind of test?

"I'll tell you what day it is."

Good.

"It's the last day of August." His mum explained, helpfully. "You're in school on the 4th of September. You've got a new bag, a pencil case and all the things you need. Do you remember, we got everything weeks ago?" She paused to look at him.

Danny looked back.

His mum folded her arms. "Well, do you remember? Do you know where it all is? Is it all ready? Will you be able to find it?"

Danny quickly said, "Yes," but he wasn't certain which question he was answering.

"And your new calculator?"

"Yes."

"And your new PE kit?"

"All sorted, Mum." Danny was on safer ground now he knew what the conversation was about. All he needed to do was reassure everyone that everything would be okay, and things would calm down. Easy.

He quickly explained that all his school things were ready, organised and handy. As he was saying all of this, he was frantically trying to remember where the pencil case and the calculator were. He'd not seen them for weeks, and it was just like his mum to demand that he bring them to the table to prove they were all sorted. He didn't need this sort of pressure at the moment.

His mum seemed satisfied. His dad was making drinks. Ellie brought the conversation back to the funny video of a cat falling into a toilet. It was a video Will had sent, and everyone thought it was hilarious.

Danny ate the rest of his tasteless pasta in silence, his mind had moved back to the Roman coins.

DANNY HAD FILLED the plastic tub with soil, buried the coins and hidden it under his bed. In the morning, they would be dirty and more believable. He'd also spent a few minutes hunting down his calculator and pencil and making sure they were in his new pencil case. This was a black and silver checked one, the old cartoon pencil case was in the box of For Sale items. He didn't want to spend his first day of secondary school being embarrassed by a cute cartoon pencil case.

He was ready for the morning, coins all sorted.

He was ready for school in five days' time, too.

There was a slight pang of annoyance about the school thing. If they had remained in his old house, he would be going to school with George and Ben. They would probably be in the same form. That would be fun. JJ would be there too, with wonky glasses, and Macka. Danny wondered if Macka would still take his dog to school. He probably wouldn't be allowed.

He thought he was beginning to miss his old mates more than ever.

For a second he allowed himself to wonder about his new school. Ellie and Will would be in Year 9. He wouldn't know anyone in Year 7 except Luke. He wasn't sure whether being there with Luke was that much of an advantage.

He hoped everything would be okay.

THIRTEEN
THE POST OFFICE

THE NEXT MORNING Danny met Luke at the gate of his house and showed him the newly dirty coins. "They look perfect," Luke said as he looked carefully at the coins. "If I was a collector I guess I would buy them."

"If you were a collector you'd probably recognise them as fakes," Danny told him. "But I'm not worried about that, from what you said I don't think Mr Jackson is an expert or anything. He probably wants something he can sell on quickly in the pub."

Luke was staring at him.

"What?" Danny stared back. "Ok, you may know the people who live here better than me. But I think I know what makes people tick. I can spot someone who knows their business, and I think Mr Jackson is a shop-keeper not an expert in ancient coins."

Luke seemed to look pale. "I hope you're right."

For all his confident words, Danny too was a little uncertain. He remembered something George had always said: "Act confident, and you're almost there." Confidence is the key. He hoped that if he had plenty of it, some might rub off on Luke. "Come on," he said and marched down the street towards the Post Office.

"What do we say to Mr Jackson?" Luke asked, "Are you going to ask for £45 straight away."

"Of course not," Danny sneered. He'd heard his dad making sales calls enough to know a few things. "Asking too early for a sale is a dead give-away. In fact," he added quizzically, "we are going to do the exact opposite."

"We are?"

"Easy." As they walked, Danny turned a little to face Luke. "Here, you be Mr Jackson. We'll rehearse. Best to be prepared."

Luke slowed down. "So, I'm Mr Jackson?"

"Yes, you start."

Luke continued thinking for a few more steps and then suddenly blurted out in a low, grumbling, old-fashioned type of voice: "What do you have there, my boy. Is it something thou' hast brought for me?"

Danny stopped and stared. "This isn't a School play. Why are you pretending to be a pirate?"

"What am I supposed to say?"

Danny sighed. They were getting close to the Post Office by now, so he knew they would have to be quick. "I'll start," he said. Then, with a slightly firmer voice said: "Oh, Mr Jackson?"

"Yes," Luke replied in a voice that was a little deeper than his usual one.

"I wondered if you could help us. We found these in the field the other day, and we don't know what they are. Do you?"

"They're coins."

"Ooh, what type of coins?"

"You know perfectly well, they're…" Luke had to stop because Danny grabbed his arm and squeezed it hard.

"I know what they are."

"But you just…"

"I know what I just said. I'm pretending. Okay?" Danny stared hard at Luke. "I'm pretending. You know, like when you pretend to be intelligent."

With that, Danny strode on more quickly, then noticed that Luke was no longer at his side. He stopped to look back. Luke was some way down the street. Standing still, looking glum.

Danny shrugged. "I'm sorry." He took a pace or two towards him. "Come on, let's just go and see Mr Jackson. No more rehearsing. The only thing is we want him to think we don't know what the coins are."

"I see."

"It's got to be his idea to think they are valuable. We don't tell him that. Okay?"

"Okay, I've got it!" It wasn't quite a yell.

WHEN THEY GOT to the Post Office, it was in darkness. The sign on the door said that on Sundays it was open from 10:00 am until 6:00 pm. Danny checked his watch; it was only 10:25.

"How come he's not open yet?"

"He sometimes opens later than it says on the weekends."

"But the sign…" Danny pointed, but Luke had turned to go. "Hey," Danny called after him. "You can't give up that easily, let's knock on the door."

Luke continued walking away, and Danny had to jog up to him to pull him back. "We should knock."

"That's what I'm going to do," Luke said. "Come on."

Danny looked puzzled. But the truth of the matter soon dawned on him as he followed Luke around the corner to the back of the row of houses. This was the path they had taken when they had the metal detector. From this side, the Post Office looked like one more house in a line of similar dark buildings. This was Fosse Lane, the end house had a green door with a number 10 on it. It was the best-maintained house of the row. Danny was surprised when Luke marched smartly up to the door and rapped hard on the shiny paint. Maybe his own confidence had started to rub off on Luke after all.

As the door opened, Danny began to wish he had

managed to save a little of the confidence for himself. What had he done?

A man's face appeared in the gap between the door and the frame. It was difficult to tell if it was the same person they had seen the other day. The man, Mr Jackson, looked like he hadn't washed or shaved. His voice was a little rougher than Danny remembered too.

"Who is it?" the man grumbled.

"It's me, Luke Ellis," Luke said brightly. His voice was a sharp thin contrast to the man's. "I've got Danny, er, er…" his voice faltered, and he turned to stare at Danny.

"Danny James," Danny said by way of help. He smiled, but he was a little upset that Luke hadn't remembered his name. Some friend he was!

"You saw us on the field yesterday. We found some Roman…" Luke had started to say. Danny could tell he was already off-script and about to ruin the plan. He pushed himself forward and blurted his words over Luke's:

"We found some strange coins. But we don't know what they are," he said with a warm smile. "We wondered if you could help us identify them." There, that ought to win him a prize from the drama department.

Mr Jackson stared blankly out at him. Then said: "Oh, yes. I remember. Come on in. I'll get my glasses."

Mr Jackson looked a little odd, but Danny was cheered by the mention of glasses. So, the old man's eyesight wasn't good. That should help. He grinned, gave Luke a friendly thump on the shoulder and followed inside.

He could see his mum was going to have a lovely birthday.

FOURTEEN

NUMBER 10 FOSSE LANE

As soon as the boys stepped out of the morning sun, they noticed a difference. The rooms at the back of the post office were dark and untidy and extremely chilly. It seemed Mr Jackson didn't like the idea of light getting inside and troubling him. All of the windows were covered with thick, grimy curtains. The room was also filled to the edges with tins and packets left over from the shop. Mr Jackson seemed to be storing hundreds of groceries and cleaning products. They were piled on every surface throughout the room.

The two boys were led through the multiple towers of packets, bottles and cans into the man's living room. Danny looked around. There was a TV in there somewhere, he could hear the sounds of an adventure film. There was also a settee, but every scrap of surface was covered with boxes of dried food and tins.

"I'd ask you to sit down," Mr Jackson said as he

reached for a light switch. "But you wouldn't manage it in here." He grinned, and Danny realised that the man must have false teeth. Or, rather, he had false teeth somewhere in the house, he sure wasn't wearing them now. Danny's grandad often had the same look when he took his teeth out; his face seemed hollow and flabby. Mr Jackson looked like that, and when he smiled, it was only a glistening wet gummy look instead of a proper smile. Danny elbowed Luke in his side to let him know he'd noticed. Luke grimaced.

Even with the light on it seemed unlikely to Danny that anyone could actually see anything clearly. The lightbulb was stained with brown ooze, and he guessed that at some stage someone in the house had been a heavy smoker.

Mr Jackson disappeared behind a curtain into another room, there was a click, and another light came on. This one, even though it was beyond a curtain, managed to give off far more light. The illumination streamed in around the edges of the dark cloth. Danny assumed this was the way into the shop. He guessed the shop would have strip lights, and this seemed to be that sort of bright white light.

Mr Jackson shuffled back into the room. "Come in here," he said, waving his arm back towards the curtained doorway. "This is my hobby."

Danny was confused, he exchanged baffled glances with Luke. This is my hobby?

The old man went back into the inner room, and

the two boys followed. A moment later they were in the middle of a room flooded with light. The contrast with the dingy, cluttered living room was eye-watering. The curtained doorway was not, as Danny had thought, a door into the shop-front, but an entrance to a completely different room. This room had three extremely bright, extremely long fluorescent tube lights. The glare was intense, and there was the recognisable low hum coming from two of the long bulbs. Then his eyes adjusted, Danny noticed that they were now standing in a small office, complete with a filing cabinet, desk, shelves and walls covered in… Danny gasped.

He stared at the walls…

He turned around slowly to check each wall in turn… They were all the same.

Everywhere he looked he could see Roman artefacts. The room was small, but there were dozens of framed maps on every wall, beneath the maps were display cases of Roman items, swords, helmets. And, of course, coins. It was like a fantastic Expert room in some museum devoted exclusively to Roman memorabilia.

Mr Jackson was a shopkeeper with a secret hobby. He was a total Roman Expert.

Danny was lost!

By the time Danny had managed to gasp a short, "Oh" sound, Mr Jackson was standing at his side. He had put on a pair of thick glasses and was holding a magnifying glass.

"Well, where are your coins?" The man chewed the words with his gummy mouth.

Danny looked away from Mr Jackson's gleaming headlight glasses. He looked briefly at the man's wobbling, hollow cheeks and then turned to search for Luke. His friend was standing some distance away, eyes wide, mouth gaping as he too looked on in stunned silence at all the Roman items in the room.

This was the end.

There was no escape.

Unless…

Danny dropped his hand to his pocket, felt the thin plastic bag with the ever so obvious fake coins inside. The edges of the coins were hard against his fingers, but all he could feel was the blood pounding in his head as he tried to think of an escape plan.

"I forgot them!"

"What?" Mr Jackson took a step back.

Danny relaxed. That was a flash of inspiration: "I meant to show them to you, but I think I left them at home." He left the coins in his pocket, brought his hands out and held his arms wide in a kind of shrug. At the same time, he started to move closer to the door.

Luke was watching him in confusion.

Almost in slow motion, Danny saw Luke open his lips to speak. There was no doubt in Danny's mind what his friend was about to say, so he shouted over his words: "Come on, Luke. We'll go and get them." He caught hold of Luke's sleeve and pulled him towards the door.

"But, they're in your pocket—"

"Come on!" Danny drowned out Luke's sentence as he pushed him out of the museum-study room. He paused momentarily at the doorway and added for Mr Jackson's benefit: "It's a wonderful collection. If we had more time, we'd love to see it properly. Thank you."

A moment later the two boys were back outside number 10 Fosse Lane. In the next minute, they were halfway down Bargate Road and heading back to Danny's house. It was some time before they both stopped running, and it was a good few minutes after that before either of them had enough breath to speak.

"Being with you is dangerous," Luke gasped when they got back to The Oaks.

"That was horrible," Danny agreed. "He would have known straight away they weren't good coins. He'd probably think we're idiots for thinking they were real. Or he would have instantly guessed we were trying to trick him. Either way, the end wouldn't have been pretty."

"No £45 then?"

"No, and we never go back to the Post Office again. Promise?"

"Promise!"

FIFTEEN
MAPS AND PLANS

THE NEXT MORNING Danny's mum made him lay out all of his school uniform.

"But Mum," Danny complained when she directed him to place everything in piles in front of the window. "I thought we had to keep this room tidy in case we had visitors."

"We can make an exception for a few days. I want to know you have everything and that you know where everything is."

There was no arguing with her. Danny's mum had her own logic, and he knew not to try to test it.

"Now, where's your sister?"

"Ellie?"

His mum put her hands on her hips and looked at him sharply, "Do you have another sister?"

"No." He grinned. "But are you saying that I have to take her to school?"

"No. She's taking you! Well… she will be with you at the bus stop. You know where that is? She'll make sure you get on and off in the right place." His mum paused, then added: "You don't have to sit with her."

"Good, because I'm not."

"You know where the bus stop is?"

"Yes, Mum."

"Do you need me, or Ellie, to draw you a map?"

"No, Mum."

"There might be days when you have to catch the bus on your own. A map would be——"

"Useful!" Danny cut in thoughtfully.

"But, there's always Luke, of course." His mum had her own thoughts. She continued talking about them, oblivious to the fact that Danny had stopped listening. "Yes, Luke can show you where to wait. And you can sit with him."

Danny's attention returned to her words again, and he winced. "I might… on some days…" He was getting more comfortable with the idea of having Luke as a friend. Of course, this may only be temporary; he might make better friends once school started.

His mum was standing looking out of the window. "He's been a good friend over the last few days, hasn't he?"

"Yes, kind of, I suppose."

"He seems to like you."

"How do you know?"

As her reply, she moved away from the window and

pointed. Outside, coming up the lane was a familiar figure.

Danny looked at his mum and then through the window at Luke.

"Go on," she said, reading his expression. "You go and play, we can finish sorting your bag later."

Danny's body tensed at the word 'play'. "I'm not five," he said.

His mum laughed. "No, but you can be back by 5:00 can't you?"

———

DANNY TOOK Luke straight into the kitchen. "I've had another idea," he said.

"Of course you have."

Danny stared at him for a moment, trying to work out if his words had been said out of admiration or irritation. He decided it wasn't admiration. Well, he would change that. He went to the book rack and pulled out a map book. "My mum was talking about getting the bus for school."

"Yes, it's easy," Luke interrupted, "You need to go down to the end of Castle Street and—"

"Don't tell. Don't tell me…" Danny waved his hands at Luke to get him to stop talking. "Mum mentioned drawing a map."

"Oh, no," Luke interrupted again. "You don't need a map, you just go down to the end of—"

Danny thrust the map book into Luke's hands. "I don't want to know," he said. "Here, look at this."

Luke stared at the book '10 Circular Walks in Derbyshire', then looked back at the shelf at all of the recipe books. "Are we baking something?"

"No, the books are all muddled up. This one just happens to be in the kitchen. Look inside." Danny wanted to show his idea to Luke. He wasn't sure why it was suddenly important to do this. It would normally have seemed more natural to just get everything done and then get Luke to help afterwards. But here he was explaining his idea before putting it into action. Weird.

"Right, look," he pointed. "There are ten different walks in here. 16 pages. This booklet costs over £8, but it's only a simple black and white set of maps."

Luke nodded, but it looked like he didn't understand. "I don't understand," he said.

Danny sighed. "This has nothing to do with school or catching buses. Forget about that. This is to do with raising money. I only have a few days left. We are going to make some map books and sell them?"

"WE?"

"Yes. You can help." Danny watched Luke think. He had caught his friend's interest but still needed to make his plan clearer. "My dad's got a set of walking books, and my mum has a photocopier. We are just putting the two together. A bit of cutting and sticking and we can easily make a map book. I'm thinking we make it A4, but fold it in half to make a nice thick A5 booklet. If we keep one walk to each page, it won't matter about the order or which map comes first. It's simple."

"We can do this?"

"Of course we can, I can type up a cover page and even add a photo of the hills around here."

Luke was carefully reading the leaflet. "But don't we have to do the walks. You know, don't we have to test them out? It says here some of these walks start or end at a pub, some are 5 miles, and some are 10. How many walks have you been on around here?"

Danny shrugged. "Oh, that's just little details. You're worrying about the tiny things. It doesn't matter. No one really reads the books in any case. I know my dad bought this walking books but he's only looked at it once or twice. It'll be fine. Don't worry."

Danny shot off to find more of his dad's walking maps. "Come on. This is going to be great."

SIXTEEN

THE PHOTOCOPIER

IN THE STUDY, his dad had a pile of boxes, and some unpacked tools were strewn on the floor.

"This looks like your bedroom," Luke observed.

Danny found a box labelled 'Bks' and hunted inside. The sound of a door opening made him look round and shout. "Dad, is that you?"

It was. The big man walked in, smiling. "Oh, hello. Are you two helping with the sorting?"

Luke said hello, but looked a little nervous.

"It's fine," Danny whispered to him. "Dad won't mind."

His dad heard him. "Dad won't mind what?"

"I know you've got some walking books in here," Danny said. "Could we borrow them?"

"You're thinking about going for a walk?" his dad looked and sounded surprised. "But you know my books aren't..." he stopped as Danny pulled something up from the bottom of the box and waved it in the air. He looked like a magician who had just found a rabbit at the bottom of a hat. His searching had moved the box to the edge of the table. Now, as he cheerfully turned to go, the box started leaning over the edge.

"No worries," Danny cried, holding a plastic bag in the air. "I've found them. A load of them. Can we borrow these?" Before his dad could respond properly, Danny had scooped Luke up and ushered him out of the room. They were down the corridor when they heard the heavy bump of the box fall onto the floor.

"Danny!" his dad called after them, but Danny had decided not to hear.

———

"RIGHT, we only need to find four or five of the most interesting walks. The ones with the best looking maps." Danny told Luke as they unwrapped the parcel of booklets and started peering through them.

They were both in the garage, sitting in a small space between more boxes and stored furniture. Beside them on a low table was an old photocopier which Danny had switched on to give it time to warm up.

While Luke hunted through the books, Danny checked the machine.

There was a small round light on the front that was blinking red, and a weird message on the screen told him it wasn't ready yet. The words should have said Wait Warming Up - but the machine was so old some of the letters on the display didn't work properly, so instead it said:

W_IT W_LMINC UP

Luke was thumbing through the map books very slowly, it seemed to Danny as if he was reading them like they are story books. He had to hurry him up. "Are you ok?" he asked.

Luke nodded, "A-Okay captain," he was making his voice sound as though it came over a radio. Danny shrugged. It seemed to him Luke could sometimes be a little silly. He grabbed the map books from him and started hunting through them himself.

Danny was doing everything now. He searched for the best walking maps while repeatedly pushing the same 'start' button on the old photocopier. He stared at the old machine, tapped the broken screen impatiently and then waited again.

A moment later, and the black and white cat they had seen outside was sniffing around just inside the door.

Danny glared at it. "I can't work with that thing in here."

"Danny, can I help?"

"Yes, take that thing outside."

"Don't you like cats?" Luke went to pick it up.

"This is more important than soppy cats," Danny said.

A few moments later, the machine clicked on. There was the gentle hum of electronics and the faint smell of dusty machinery warming up as the old photocopier came to life. The little digital screen told him it was:

RE_DY

Danny tried to sort the maps out as quickly as he could. Behind him, Luke was holding onto the cat and glancing around the room. Danny wisely decided he didn't want to spoil his dad's books, so he quickly copied a few map pages. His idea was to cut these down and re-photocopy them, but he'd forgotten to bring any scissors and didn't want to go back into the house in case questions were asked. So he quickly tore the copied maps to size.

Danny then arranged the map pieces on the glass platen of the photocopier. Luke was sitting watching him. "Danny, can I do anything to help?"

"It's fine," Danny was working furiously on his own.

Suddenly the cat jumped out of Luke's arms and landed next to the photocopier.

Danny looked from the cat to Luke. Then, shrugging in disgust, he picked the cat up and marched outside. Putting it out on the street wouldn't work since it would just come back. He thought for a moment, then had an idea.

When he returned empty-handed, he was grinning.

Luke waited.

"That's sorted it," Danny clapped his hands together.

"What have you done?"

"I've locked it in my dad's car—"

"You can't. It won't be able to breathe."

"I'm not stupid; I opened the driver's window a little. Come on, let's get on with this."

Luke shook his head and settled for offering a word of advice, or pointing out if something wasn't quite straight on the photocopier glass. The machine, as well as having a dodgy LCD screen, was only making faint copies. The newly copied map sheets were faint grey rather than black and white. Still, they were reasonably legible, so Danny pressed on.

They'd assembled a booklet of 6 maps across 8 pages when Luke asked: "What about the cover? Can you print something on your computer? I could design something if you wanted."

Danny shook his head. He could have designed a cover himself. But he felt he needed to do this in a rush so hunted around the garage for a more efficient solution.

Half an hour later, the two boys emerged from the gloom of the garage with a stack of booklets. Danny had found an old stencil kit in a box of stationery. That, together with a couple of felt pens, had given him a half-decent cover. Luke agreed that it had a strange childish look. Danny had argued that this type of cover would "Make it stand out from the rest of the map books."

Luke pulled a face. But Danny was confident.

Everything was working out wonderfully. They would be ready to sell the map books first thing in the morning.

"Right after breakfast. You meet me here. Ok?"

Luke nodded and the two parted company.

As Luke passed the car on the drive, he called out to Danny and pointed.

Of course, the cat, how could he forget? Danny didn't like cats much, but he wasn't going to leave one locked in a car all night. He let it go and was pleased to see it hurtling off across the garden and away to the neighbouring houses.

There, that was his good deed for the day. Tomorrow, he was bound to reap the rewards.

About £45 should do nicely.

SEVENTEEN

SOME OF OUR FAVOURITE WALKS

THE NEXT MORNING Luke walked to The Oaks to meet Danny. He was beginning to warm to this new friendship. At first, Luke had thought Danny was a little unfriendly, too fast to judge and argumentative. But now he was starting to like him. He just hoped they could agree to do things together. Last evening in the garage had not been such a fun time. He remembered that everything he had done had been criticised or changed.

He met up with Danny just as arranged, right outside his house.

Danny seemed pleased to see him and insisted on showing him the finished maps again as they walked into town.

Luke admired the careful way the pages had been stapled but was now even less happy with the front cover than he had been the night before.

"What's that?"

"Ah," Danny grinned. "I thought it was a good idea to write £6 on the front."

Luke pulled a face, the writing was crude and rushed.

"We will only charge £5," Danny said quickly. "The £6 is there so we can say we are offering a discount."

Luke wasn't worried about the price, it was the awful, rushed writing. He sighed, working together might be harder than he thought.

"It's fine," Danny said, "Don't worry about it. These will sell like hotcakes. The next thing we need to work on is the location. That's the first rule of selling things, get a good location."

Luke knew that Colin, Danny's dad, was a sales-man. So he was sure Danny knew what he was talking about. After a quick chat, they decided that the best place to sell maps would be in the middle of the town. "We can stand at the end of the car park," Luke explained. "That will be a great place. Lots of people there today."

Without any argument or further discussion, they headed off. Danny seemed happy to follow his advice, and Luke was pleased about that.

The car park was also on the opposite side of town from the post office, which - as Danny had been quick to point out - was a very good thing.

When they got into the town, they chose to stand

near the Car Park ticket machine. This also had the good fortune to be directly opposite a camping shop.

Danny spotted the shop immediately. "That's where we need to be," he said. "Let's go and stand near there, we might catch likely walkers."

It took them twenty minutes of smiling and waving at people before they had their first proper customer.

A young man and woman with a baby in a buggy had stopped. They only stopped to tuck in a blanket that had come away from the baby's feet. But it seemed to Luke that Danny hadn't noticed the blanket. He probably thought some mysterious force of nature had brought them to him.

Luke could almost hear Danny's thoughts. '*This is fate, Luke, my good friend. Fate, I tell you, and fate is going to bring us £5.*' Luke shook his head when he realised his imagination had made a mistake. No, Danny would probably be thinking: '*Fate is going to bring **me** £5.*'

At his side, Danny was already pushing a map booklet towards the couple.

The woman was bending and fussing over the baby so she ignored him, but the man smiled and glanced at the booklet.

"Have you made these?" he took the booklet, looked quickly through it and pointed out different pages to his wife. The baby, close to Danny's knees began making gurgling sounds.

"They are some of our favourite walks." Danny

said, "We thought we should share them with other people. There are some great views."

Luke was surprised at the way Danny said these things so casually. For a moment he thought about trying to stop him, but he knew it would be useless.

The man hunted through the pages, got to the back of the book and passed it to his wife. She was not as interested as he was and immediately gave it back to Danny. As she did this, Luke heard Danny say: "It's part of a school project. We are also raising money for charity?" Luke frowned, that was a double forced attack. He knew that the words 'school project' almost always worked magic with adults. Of course, the 'money for charity' part was originally his idea.

However crafty the words might have been, they weren't about to work on this couple.

"It's a nice idea," the man said, "but we don't plan to go too far outside the town. Not with this." He pointed to the buggy and the baby. "Maybe if we come back in a few months. Thanks." And he pushed the buggy past them.

Luke shrugged. "Hey, that was good, you nearly had a sale."

LATER IN THE DAY, they seemed to have more luck with their map booklets.

A small group of people had gathered around. It

seemed to Danny that one or two came up to talk to them and then two more came to see what the first two were looking at and the group grew bigger. After only a few minutes there was quite a crowd of people around them. Danny was quite pleased about this and was in full 'sales' mode. He was disappointed though that each time he announced what the map books were for a few people left.

A moment later and a shout rang out.

Danny looked around.

"It's the man from the camping shop," Luke said. "Oh, he looks a bit upset. Come on, we better go." With that, Luke set off at a fast run.

Danny had no option but to do the same. For a moment, the crowd of people around them looked like they were going to run after them, but instead, the group faded into the rest of the shoppers on the street.

As he looked over his shoulder, Danny noticed that a lot of the people were heading into the camping shop. That should keep the man happy he thought. Just a shame they didn't buy one of my maps first.

The two boys headed off, away from the crowd.

Just ahead of him, Luke stopped. Danny ran up, and the two boys stood there panting. That was when they got their first real customer.

EIGHTEEN
RAY, TAKE YOUR HAT OFF

By ACCIDENT, they had settled directly outside Reeds the Opticians. At that exact moment, an elderly man came out of the opticians and almost bumped into them.

"Oh, sorry boys, excuse me," the old man said.

Danny immediately apologised too, partly because his mum had told him always to treat elderly people with great respect, and partly because it was his fault. He had suddenly stopped right outside the door.

Before Danny could say anything, Luke had hissed in his ear. "Let's keep the lies to a minimum. Okay?"

Danny nodded. By now the old man had been joined by an even older woman.

Danny handed the map booklet to the old man. As he did, he noticed how soft his wrinkled fingers were.

The old man switched his bag from one hand to the

other. Beside him, the old lady leant forwards as they looked through the pages.

"It's a little faint," the man said to Danny. "The writing, I mean. A bit hard to see."

His wife pushed in at his side. She shouted a little: "Put your glasses on, Ray. I can see it."

The man, Ray, looked at Danny.

"We can sell it for £5." Danny was saying.

Ray looked at his wife. "Irene, he's just like our Tommy," he said.

"Yes," Irene said, rather loudly. "Very keen and bright."

Danny wasn't clear what they were talking about. "Is it too bright here, we can move out of the sun." He took a few steps back, encouraging them further into the cool shadow of the shop. "Let me tell you more about the walks in here."

IRENE WATCHED her husband as he held the map. His hands were shaking again, and she knew he couldn't possibly see the print properly.

"Let me look," she said, taking over the map and leafing through its pages. Her eyesight was sharp, as sharp as her tongue, Ray would usually tell any new people they met. The map book looked useful, although some place names seemed a little odd. She didn't think Castleton was anywhere near here.

Still, the two young boys seemed honest enough.

She looked carefully at their calm, open faces as they chatted away to Ray. Now they were reminding him the price was lowered to £5 today. Just for today - a one-off special offer - she chuckled at that. The words reminded her of her daughter's husband. She didn't like the words, didn't much like her daughter's husband for that matter. I hope they got those ideas off the TV, she thought. The boys seemed too nice to get pulled into salesmen's ways. Usually don't trust chaps who talk like that, don't believe a word of it. Here though, it seemed natural.

These boys were too young to be villains like her Son-in-Law.

She'd made up her mind. "Let's take it," she said, poking Ray in the ribs.

"Eh," he looked at her but hadn't heard.

"These two young lads have wasted too much time talking to you already." She looked at her husband again. "Ray, take your hat off."

Then turning to Danny and Luke, she added. "He can't hear a thing with his hat on." The boys laughed.

By this time Ray had removed his hat and was looking with a slightly puzzled expression at his wife.

She smiled at him and then laughed loudly as she turned once more to Danny and Luke. "He can't hear a thing with it off either."

The boys smiled politely, and Irene was pleased she had entertained them. "He's deaf you know. He might nod and look like he knows what you are saying, but he's as deaf as my stick. And he can't see without his glasses."

She turned back and smiled at Luke, then moved her gaze to Danny. There was something about this young boy, she thought. Yes, Ray had been right, she could see the sweet glint in the boy's eyes, and it did remind her of her grandson, Tommy.

Then, when she saw the boys' faces cloud with disappointment, she said to them, and to Ray: "We'll take it. And, since I don't think it's fair to take advantage of you two, we'll give you the proper price. If it says £6 on the front here." She tapped at the corner of the folded map booklet. "Then it's worth £6." After that, Irene stopped and waited. Ray didn't take the hint, so she jabbed him sharply in the side again. She noticed with a faint smile that the boys thought that was funny.

Ray, however, didn't. But he did at least manage to realise what she wanted and hunted in his pocket for his wallet.

A moment later and Irene was the proud owner of Danny and Luke's map.

"Thank you, you two. And good luck with selling the rest of your little books." Irene said as the money changed hands.

The boys thanked them repeatedly and then headed off in the opposite direction with their £6.

"Come on," Irene said, pulling Ray. "Let's get a cup

of tea and then look at the map properly. I could do a nice sit down before we go for a good walk."

Danny couldn't believe his luck. He'd made a sale.

He also felt just a little uncertain about the whole thing.

"Thank you," he called after the couple. He suddenly felt the need to give them something for the £6. It was almost as though the flimsy photocopied pages weren't worth the money. Which, he had to admit, they certainly weren't.

"Thank you," he said again. It was the only thing he could offer.

NINETEEN
APPROACHING TROUBLE

DANNY WOULD NEVER ADMIT IT, but his insides were clawing at him. He rubbed his stomach as though it were a real upset kind of pain. It felt like that time he and George had got hold of a bucket of crab apples. They'd munched them all down and then regretted it. The pain now was the same. A stomach-churning roller-coaster feeling made up of a bad taste and the feelings of guilt. "I think we tricked that old couple."

"Well, I suppose we did." Luke offered. His words weren't helping.

Danny frowned. "I'm telling myself the money was for a good cause."

"What?"

"It was for a good cause. My mum's happiness is a **very good cause**. If that old lady had a son or daughter they would want to look after them and put their mum first, wouldn't they? That's all I'm doing."

"Yes," Luke cheered a little at that. "You could put it that way."

"And no one's getting hurt are they?"

Danny watched as Luke shook his head. Good, there was some agreement there. He was beginning to think that the friendship between him and Luke was starting to work. Maybe it had moved from being a new friend to being a close one. Of course, he wasn't going to say any of this to Luke.

Feeling a little happier, the boys wandered out of the centre of town. They found a busy corner on the hill near the hairdressers which they thought would be a popular place for selling their maps. However, after standing and smiling at dozens of people, Danny had only managed to interest one other visitor in his maps, and then they only looked quickly and walked away.

"This worked better with the elderly." Luke reminded him.

"We've been here hours," Danny said. He sighed, "This is a waste of time. It's too slow."

"Oh no, we better run," Luke said sharply in his ear.

"I don't think running will help—" Danny stopped abruptly. He could see what Luke had spotted moments before. At the corner of the street below them, between Evans Greengrocers and the Lady Langly's Hat store was a familiar figure. No, as he looked, he realised it was much worse. There were **two** familiar figures. The first was Luke's brother, William, not that threatening.

The second was Danny's sister, Ellie. And if Ellie caught up with them she could twist his plans and make it seem as though he was a master criminal. The couple were walking directly towards them.

Danny watched carefully as his sister and her boyfriend (should he call William that?) slowly came up the hill. If Ellie were in any way normal, Danny thought, or even observant, she was bound to see him and Luke. Of course, Ellie only had eyes for William and seemed to be walking almost sideways, her body and her face turned so she could watch William. Danny had the idea she looked like some lovesick crab.

The two boys exchanged glances and immediately dashed down a side street next to the hairdressers.

———

Panting, Luke glanced back up the alleyway, pleased that they had avoided the approaching trouble "I'm guessing they were going into the cafe. My brother loves his food."

That seemed to satisfy Danny since he looked more cheerful. "Right, if they are busy, we'll be safe for a bit. Let's get back to where there are more people." Danny tapped the pack of maps. "If we're careful we can sell some more of these this afternoon."

Luke was less sure. For one, it seemed that it had taken over three hours to sell their first map. For two, he had sensed Danny had been upset by the sale. True, it seemed he had got over that now. But he'd also felt they had cheated the old couple. Also, and this was easier to sort, he was beginning to feel hungry. For once, he wished he was spending the afternoon with his brother. A sandwich and a cold drink would be most welcome right now.

When they got back to the middle of the town, it was still busy with tourists. Luke hated coming into town normally. It was so boring, but now he had a reason to be there.

"Should we go over by the library?" Danny was pointing.

Luke wasn't impressed with that, the library was always a dull place. It was also the one place tourists avoided. Next to the library though was the entrance to the indoor market. That looked more promising. He told Danny, and they crossed the road and set up 'shop' beside the entrance.

Several dozen people walked past them in the first few minutes. One sporty looking man in a tracksuit even stopped briefly to look at the maps, but he jogged away again before the boys could start to sell.

Luke hoped they would have better luck soon.

COLIN JAMES STOPPED PAINTING, stepped back and admired the kitchen. He had just painted the last corner of the last wall and was delighted to have reached the end of this decorating job. He smiled to himself as he surveyed the great work. The room was perfect, a little smelly with the paint, but perfect. The walls looked smooth and even, and the ceiling was finished. Now, there was a frustrating problem with the sink. He would have to replace the pipe and move that bucket. But that would take longer than he had left today. Another couple of days, he hoped, and the kitchen would be finished. Longer than they had planned, but only the plumbing problems were holding them up now.

He placed the paintbrush back in the tray and took all the tools out to the garage. A quick clean up and then a sandwich. Cheese and pickle. Thick white slices of bread and cheddar cheese. He'd seen some in the fridge that morning. There were some nice biscuits too. He promised himself a couple of biscuits with a cup of tea.

The clean-up involved replacing the paint tins and tools. He decided to do this as quickly as possible since the sight of the untidy garage always irritated him. Inside, he pushed past the mess of toys, garden equipment and untidy boxes and placed the painting things back as close to the back wall as possible. It would do, at least they were out of the house.

He turned to go when something bright and glowing caught his eye.

A burning red dot near the floor. For an instant, his mind thought of a glowing cigarette. His mum used to smoke dozens of cigarettes a day. That was when she was younger, and fitter. This looked just like that, he bent to look more closely and then realised it was a tiny LED light. The photocopier. Why was that turned on, Ellie wouldn't use it, and he knew that Helen wouldn't use it in here. If she wanted to copy something she would have moved the machine out into the house. Or asked him to move it. Yes, that was more likely.

He lifted the copier lid and immediately saw a collection of papers.

Forgetting about the tidying job and the sandwich he had promised himself, he picked up the papers and took them outside into the sunlight.

Now he could see them properly, he recognised the handwriting. He also had a pretty good idea what they were for.

"Danny!"

TWENTY
I'LL BE RIGHT HOME

DANNY WAS CROSS; Luke seemed to be spending most of the time playing with two puppies. Danny, without any real help, was trying to sell the map to the lady with the dogs. She was partially interested, but it seemed from her question she wanted to know where the money was going.

"Is it for a charity," she said, turning the map over in her hand. "It doesn't say anything about a charity here."

Danny thought quickly. "It's not for a formal charity, but it is to enable someone to repair an item of value."

"Oh," the lady looked unhappy. The dogs were making snuffling noises and twisting around on their leads as Luke constantly tapped them on their heads. Danny, like the lady, was unimpressed. Dogs weren't high on his list of things he liked. He regretted standing here, it was hard to sell things, particularly when your assistant (that's how he thought of Luke) doesn't do anything to help.

Just then, Danny's phone buzzed and took his attention away from the potential customer. He answered it quickly and heard his dad's voice. There was no doubt who it was. There was a lot of voice to hear.

His attention was now totally on trying to repair whatever situation he was about to find himself in. And the lady, who was proving hard to please and who may never have bought anything in any case, started to fade from of his mind.

"Ah. Yes Dad. Yes, we did." Danny said in a hollow low voice. He didn't even notice the lady had gone, taking her unwilling puppies with her, until Luke returned to stand at his side like some dark unhelpful shadow.

"Yes, Dad. Er, yes. We will."

Luke was starting to move away, so Danny thrust out a hand to grab him back. This was a large slice of trouble, and he felt it would be better if it were shared. "Yes, Dad," he said the same two words for the third time. And then, just for luck, once more: "Yes, Dad... I'll be right home now." He killed the phone conversation with a stab of the button and looked at Luke.

Luke looked back.

"This could be bad," Danny said. "My dad's found a copy of the map on the photocopier, and he's not happy." He fell silent for a moment. Not happy at all, he thought. But it seemed the problem was not about them using the photocopier without asking, but there was something wrong with the map, and (of course) with the price, they'd hastily added to the front. What was it with adults and prices. They never seemed happy to see them.

"He doesn't like the idea of us trying to sell maps that don't belong to us," he explained as they hurried back through the town.

The market entrance was at the bottom end of the street, so the turning back to Bargate Road was only minutes away. Less than ten minutes back to home then. It would cheer Dad up if they got back really quickly; he'd realise that they were treating his annoy-ance seriously. Of course, the unfortunate side-effect of this 'getting back quickly' idea was that it brought the trouble a whole lot sooner than necessary.

For a second, Danny thought of going up the hill and the long way round. But realised that in the end, this would not be the healthy option.

"Come on," he said as he jogged down the street, "Let's get this over with."

TWENTY-ONE

THE FAINT GLIMMER OF PRIDE

"I'm sorry, Dad," Danny was saying.

It was the third time he'd said the same thing, but he was too worried to be counting. "I guess we didn't think."

"What?" His dad, full of annoyance, wasn't listening.

"I'm sorry." (Fourth time.) "I guess we didn't think."

His dad had clearly prepared what he wanted to say, and he was going to say it. Danny realised that his own words were like wallpaper in a noisy room.

"You didn't think," his dad roared. "The information here isn't yours to sell." He waved the maps at Danny. "You can't just photocopy maps and go around selling them. How many people have you pestered today?"

Danny started to answer, but his dad had the next part of his speech already loads and firing at him.

"Did anyone see you? Did the police see you? If you'd been stopped by the police, you would have been in trouble. Real trouble. Do you know you need a licence to sell things in the streets? You can't just do it. You just didn't think." There was a pause while his dad regained his breath.

Behind him, Danny could sense Luke was shifting from foot to foot.

"How many of these have you sold?" Danny's dad thumped the stack of maps Danny had given him. "Eh. How many?"

"Just one…" Danny muttered quietly.

From behind him, a voice added: "…to a lovely old couple we met in the street."

Danny winced. Luke always seemed to be helpful in the most unhelpful ways.

His dad seemed to shrink a little as his body relaxed. "Ah, one. Just one. That's a good thing. But you know what you need to do now, don't you?"

From the way he had asked it seemed to Danny that his dad had total confidence in his ability to give the right answer. In all truth, however, he was struggling to come up with a good response. After a few seconds, he decided that the best thing to do was to nod slowly.

"Well?"

Er… Danny had 101 ideas but didn't think any of them would fit the expectations his dad had. Luckily, things were put on hold when another voice shouted.

"What is all this about?" Helen was coming out of the front of the house, she looked first at him and then at his dad. "Colin, what is this? What has he done?"

Danny's inside shrivelled a little. Great. That's just great, he thought. Mum comes outside, her arms filled with books and immediately decides I've done something wrong.

"Danny here, love, has started a brand-new business venture."

"Oh," his mum looked momentarily as though she was going to be proud, but then sensed that the tone of his dad's voice indicated that Dannys' endeavours were not good. Colin continued by giving a full, if (Danny thought) slightly overexcited account, of what had happened.

Hidden in among the long list of bad things he had done, Danny was surprised to learn something about having emptied the biscuit tin, too.

The faint glimmer of pride that had momentarily shot over his mum's face was now rapidly replaced by a dark, gloomy look. He recognised this well and knew that it was the kind of look that could easily combat a nuclear explosion.

"I'm sorry, Mum." Danny decided that prevention would be better than cure. He was speaking about the maps and old people and money. In his mind, he had laid the biscuit problem to one side. He would have to deal with that later. And in any case, deep down inside him, there was a small part of his mind that insisted that her pride had been the right emotion. After all, he had just turned a pile of old papers and maps into cash. And given more time he could make more money. He wondered how much money his dad had managed to 'make' that morning.

Their disgusted looks made it seem as though his actions had been criminal. It wasn't as if he had been photocopying £5 notes directly on the machine (although, that may well be an idea for another day).

During all of this time, the words Luke had said had been playing on his dad's mind, for he suddenly moved his gaze away from Danny and turned it on Luke. "You say you sold a map to an old couple?" he frowned. "How old?"

Luke jumped. He was still standing some brave distance behind Danny. "At least 100."

"They weren't." Danny snapped. He remembered his gran and her recent birthday. "They were like gran. About 70 or 80."

"You gave this map to two 80-year-olds?" his mum said.

"Yes, Mum. But we sold it to them."

"For £6!" Luke still wasn't helping.

"You sold them this map?" his dad stressed the words carefully. Then, in a moment of reckless drama looked heavenward and sighed.

Helen stared at her husband. "What is it?"

"It's worse than you think. Look!" Colin gave her the map and flicked to an inside page. They both peered inside. Then slowly, together, like a two-headed robot, they raised their heads and glared at Danny.

There weren't any laser beams coming out of their eyes, but Danny gulped.

Questions flew.

Mum: "Since when has Lathkill Dale been near here?"

Dad: "Don't you know how dangerous this is?"

Mum: "You could have put those old people in danger."

Dad: "Did they go for a walk following one of your maps? I hope not."

Danny: "—"

Mum: "What?"

Danny stopped trying to speak. He moved forward to look at the map. "I know the print isn't easy to read."

"That's not the problem." Helen was almost shouting. "The problem is that these aren't maps of anywhere near here. You've photocopied maps from the Derbyshire Dales. If anyone tries to follow these maps round here, they'll get totally lost. Don't you see?"

Danny did see. He also remembered that Luke had helped him. Luke had been there when they were sorting the maps. Luke had... He looked around and saw that his close friend Luke was now a distant friend. Really distant, like 200 metres away, and moving fast.

He decided the best thing to do was join him.

WHEN HELEN LOOKED up from the map again, she realised her son had gone.

"Danny——"

TWENTY-TWO

ARE THEY SAFE?

DANNY RAPIDLY CAUGHT up with Luke. After all, he was a better runner. But the two boys didn't speak. Danny, partly because he was out of breath, and partly because he was deep in thought.

This was the end, he decided. His life was a miserable mess. Not just losing his old friends, not just moving to a new school, a new home, a new town. But this was a mess: He'd tricked two nice old people with a map that turned out to be dangerous. He'd made them pay £6 for it, and then sent them off into the hills without any possible clue as to how to get back.

"How cold does it get on these hills?"

"It can be deadly," Luke said. "When the mist falls, walkers have been lost for hours. Some people have died from being too cold or hungry."

"Thanks, mate. That's really cheered me up."

"It's true."

"You know what else is true?" Danny marched ahead grimly. "We've sent that couple out here with a map that doesn't work. What if one of the paths takes them up a cliff and drops them off the end of it?"

Luke sighed. "I hadn't thought **about** that. But don't worry, it would take them over a day to walk to the top of the nearest cliff."

"So, are they safe?"

"Well, apart from the cold there are quite a lot of old mine-shafts. People have fallen—"

"What!"

Luke turned and slowed his pace. "Do you even think they'll go for a walk? They looked very old."

"Old people **do** walk **about**, you know. And, did you notice the woman had a pair of those walking-poles?"

"My dad says most people just use those for wandering around town."

Danny shrugged.

"My dad says people with walking-poles rarely take them off the tarmac."

"Maybe so, but we don't know that they haven't gone for a walk in the hills." Danny pulled a booklet out of his pocket. "Here, I saved a map. They were looking at the one on page 4, see this one. We'll try to follow it."

"But your mum said the map was wrong."

"It doesn't match the paths around here, but if they

tried to follow it, we should too." Danny pointed to a line at the top of the map, "Look. We need to start from the top of Cross Street and go along a path."

"There isn't a Cross street in town!"

"No, but there is Castle Street, didn't the man, Ray, have bad eyesight. Maybe they saw Castle Street and thought it was the right one. Come on, let's pretend we're the old couple following this map and see where it takes us."

"I haven't got my glasses."

"What?" Danny looked at Luke who was walking in a crooked, bent up way and groaning to himself.

"I didn't mean 'imitate them'. Let's just walk the path and see. Come on, stop being an idiot. This could be serious."

The boys walked on, along Castle street and into North Lane, then onto a footpath. A sign said 'Keen Valley' and pointed towards the mountain beyond the hills. A valley, that sounded like easy walking.

After a few minutes, Danny spotted someone in the distance. "Is that the old woman with a stick?" He urged Luke to follow where he was pointing.

There was a distant figure walking across a field waving a stick along the ground.

Luke immediately started to laugh. It was a giggle that made him bend almost double. Then the giggle turned into a choking noise.

"You know who it is?" Luke coughed the words out as he stood upright again and tried to wipe tears from his eyes. "It's not an old woman. It's Mr Jackson from the Post Office. Look at him. He's only been and bought himself a metal detector."

After that, they took a shady path out of town.

They set a good pace, heading North again. Danny was holding the map and insisted the direction was 'Upward'. They followed the route drawn on the map although they both knew that it couldn't possibly be the same footpath on the ground. After a few hundred yards it became obvious that the map didn't match the countryside around them.

At the top of How Lane they crossed over and headed West ('Left' as Danny called it), here the map managed to agree with the real landscape for a while. Just by chance, there was a narrow stony path in roughly the right place heading in roughly the right direction. However, a little further on and things quickly came unstuck.

The map said South across a field, the path they were on only continued West and then a gentle turn towards the North. If they followed the written direc-tions, they would end up wading neck deep into a small lake.

Luke took the map from Danny. "Do you think the old couple tried to cross here?"

"Ray and Irene." Danny reminded him. "Perhaps we should think of them as real people."

Luke, having been corrected, tried again: "Do you think Ray and Irene…" he paused to stifle a laugh, "…

tried to cross here?" He pulled a pencil out of his pocket to write on the map.

"I hope not," Danny scanned the water's surface in case there were any bodies floating nearby. "I guess they just carried on along this path… What are you doing?"

Luke was scratching lines on the map. "Correcting it."

Danny frowned, and Luke put the pencil back in his pocket. He marched ahead and studiously looked at the ground. It looked like he was upset, but then it became obvious that he was looking for something. Luke was on his hands and knees, inspecting the dusty soil on the path.

"What are you doing? Get up."

"I'm looking for tracks. Don't you see?" Luke pointed to the narrow path they were trying to follow. "If they came this way there should be signs of the old lady's fancy walking-pole things. I'm looking for foot-prints with little dimples on either side."

That was an interesting idea. And Danny was suitably impressed. However, he doubted that the fragile birdlike Irene would make any indentations on the ground with her sticks.

The path hugged the side of the lake for a while as they walked on in the afternoon sun. Later it diverted them towards a group of trees. The map knew nothing of the trees or the lake, and then the real path took them up a hill that the paper one could not show.

At the top of the rise, the two boys stopped and

looked around. Danny wondered if they could make out the shape of two people standing some way off in the distance, but he realised after staring hard that it was only the remains of an old set of gate posts.

This was a good vantage point from which to survey the land, but there were no walkers anywhere to be seen. Sheep dozed in a nearby field and birds hovered overhead, but no other people, old or young.

"I can't see them anywhere," Danny said, and he checked his phone. There was a text message from his dad to say they should come back. Danny texted that they would look for another hour and then turn back.

"Let's keep following the real path for a little longer." He told Luke

"Yes, it heads up to that bigger hill," Luke pointed. "That's Spital Mountain. I've been for picnics up there in the past, it's quite a walk, but we'll be high enough to see them from up there."

Spital didn't sound especially appealing, but it was the other word which gave Danny more concern. "Mountain!" He looked up at what seemed to be a huge, grey, tree-lined wall heaving high into the sky. "You want to go up to the top of that?"

"It's not a proper mountain, that's just its name. It's not as bad as it looks."

"Do you think someone in their 80s would make it?"

"Possibly. If they walked real slow."

"They'd have to walk slow. I think I'll have to walk slow."

They set off again. Luke in the front this time, leading the way like an excited scout leader doing bushcraft.

The path grew wilder and more overgrown. In places, it almost totally disappeared under weeds and bushes.

As far as Danny was concerned, the situation was growing desperate.

TWENTY-THREE
THIS IS AWFUL

THE PATH HAD THINNED AGAIN, so they had to walk in single file when Luke suddenly let out a shout of pain and dropped to the ground. He was gripping his leg and crying out in agony. Danny guessed he'd been bitten by a snake or shot with an arrow or something equally deadly. "What's is it?" he shouted the question. He had decided to keep his distance in case his snake idea was the right one.

"My leg, my leg."

That's helpful information. "I can see you've hurt your leg, is it a bite, or a cut, or... what?"

"I've been nettled," Luke cried out. He was trying to stand now, still holding his right leg with his left hand as he scrambled upwards. He looked like a three-legged elephant trying to get out of a bath. Danny watched and told himself not to laugh.

Luke was lashing out with his good leg at some

bushes on the right-hand side of the path. He kicked and trampled on them as if he wanted to make sure the nettle had been well and truly taught a lesson for attacking him.

After a moment of this kicking, he stopped and stared at Danny, still out of breath.

"Are you happy now?" Danny asked.

"No." And he jumped up and down three more times to flatten the sorry plant.

"Come on, we'll look for a dock leaf. My mum says you have to rub a nettle sting with a dock leaf to make it feel better."

"I know," Luke said angrily. "I know what to do with nettle stings."

Danny had reached him on the path by now. "Then come on then, let's get on with it." He half pushed Luke forward, and they continued up the slight incline cutting through the narrowing overgrown path. Danny was still stepping carefully on the left of the path to avoid any remaining live nettles Luke hadn't thrashed to death.

A little while later they found a clump of dock plants and Luke rubbed a leaf on his leg. The nettle had managed to penetrate his jeans and his sock. He crumpled the dock leaf up and jammed it down his sock.

They walked on.

They stopped again.

"What is it now?" Danny almost bumped into Luke.

"My leg's itching," Luke was hunting in his pocket for something. Danny sighed and considered clambering around to be the one in the lead, but he didn't want to have to climb into the long weeds to get around Luke. There could be nettles, or…

"Are there any snakes in this area?"

Luke, who had dug the pencil out of his pocket again, looked at him. "This is North Wales," he said, "Not the outback in Australia. There are a few snakes like grass snakes or adders. But nothing to worry about. Adders are venomous, but they'll be more scared of you than you are of them."

"I wouldn't bank on it," Danny said. "But I was wondering about the old couple's safety."

"Irene and Ray," Luke corrected him with a smile as he jabbed the pencil down his sock.

Danny watched him prod at his ankle. He remembered when he had broken his right arm a few years ago, he knew just how annoyingly itchy the sweaty inside of a cast could become. He watched Luke scrub at his leg with the rubber end of the pencil. Then, he quickly became tired of waiting. "Come on, we're here to help save those old folk. Not to play around in the nettles."

The further they walked the more awkward the heather and gorse came. The gorse, in particular, was a threat to the lower limbs. Several times Danny had found he needed to hop to one side or the other to avoid being scratched to death by the thick needles on the bushes.

"This is awful." Luke said, "How much further do we have to go?"

"I've sent my dad a message to say we'll turn back at five o'clock. But, of course, we ought to stay out here until we find them." Danny knew it was a useless thing to say. But he also knew he needed words. Saying something, anything, stopped the silent emptiness of the mountain from swallowing them. "We have to get back."

"Should we try shouting?" Luke cupped his hands to his mouth and cried out, "Irene, Ray. Are you there? Irene. Ray…"

He stopped when Danny thumped him on the arm. "You sound like you're calling a couple of dogs in for their tea."

They walked on in silence for another two minutes, before Luke found something else to complain about: "I'm hungry."

Danny looked at him. "We have to find them. We're responsible. We sent them out here—"

Luke interrupted him and emphasised his words carefully: "**You** sent them out here," he said. "**You** printed the maps!"

Danny grunted. "Thanks! That's friendly."

They stumbled on. The light was fading twice as fast as normal because of the thick mist enveloping all around them. The ground and the sky were merging into one hazy grey blanket. Danny blinked hard, it was almost as though his eyes couldn't focus on anything anymore.

As they made progress, the ground grew more and more lumpy and uneven. Large holes lay everywhere like leg traps waiting to catch them when they fell.

What time was it? He checked his phone. It was just after 5:00. Time to turn back.

The phone had more news for him, though. The symbol which showed a connection to a network was blank. No signal. What if they needed help?

"Luke, do you have your phone with you?" As soon as he'd asked the question Danny sensed a weird moment at his side. Something heavy dropping to the floor.

There was a scream.

TWENTY-FOUR
DON'T TOUCH IT!

HELEN JAMES PUT the phone down and turned around. A collection of faces stared back. "The police are contacting the mountain rescue." Her voice wobbled as she spoke, she was trying not to cry.

Colin jumped up, "What!" He had his coat in his hands and started to pull it on. He was heading for the door.

"We have to stay here," Helen said. "The police insisted that we stay here. We can't do anything." She put both hands on the kitchen table, lent forward and breathed deeply. It was hard to focus on the words. "The last thing they need is more people wandering around on the mountainside." Her voice faltered again, and Colin moved away from the door and rushed to her side.

Around the table, Ellie, William and his mum, Susan, all continued staring in silence. Helen reached out and gripped Ellie's shoulder to reassure her. "It'll be okay."

She turned back to her husband, watching his expression. It was clear he wanted to be out there looking. "We stay by the phone. They're the experts."

Colin's face was grim, but he nodded. "They better find them."

"They will."

At the mention of a mobile phone, William raised his hand, just like he was in school. "Luke has his new phone with him. If he was in trouble, he'd use it." He looked at his mum for encouragement.

Susan Ellis was sitting quietly at his side, she looked carefully at his face and then turned away. "You know these mountains Will. There's no mobile signal when you get past the trees on Fox Lane." Her voice broke off, and everyone could see her shoulders gently shaking. "It's dark and late now. Let's just hope they get to shelter."

Colin couldn't keep still, he picked up his coat and headed for the door again. Helen glared at him and then relaxed when she saw he was only hanging it on the hook behind the door. He'd listened to her.

She thought of Danny and wished he'd listened too.

"Mum," Ellie suddenly blurted out. "What about the old couple who took Danny's map?"

The reply came from Colin, "Don't worry, love. Come on, you can help me make everyone a cup of tea."

Helen stared through the kitchen window. Outside, the fields, hills and mountains were all washed over with a cold, bleak darkness. She knew what the police had said on the phone. They'd sounded confident. She tried to sound the same. "They'll find them, that's what they do."

She just hoped she was right.

———

THE SCREAM WAS STILL ECHOING in the misty darkness. Danny took a deep breath and turned to look. The blurry shape that had been his friend at his side now seemed to have changed into a small blurry lump on the ground.

The awkward dark shape moved slightly, and Luke gave out another cry. Then he stopped and made a sobbing noise.

"Where are you?" Danny called.

More sobbing.

"Luke, it can't be that bad."

"It is. It is."

The darkness was folding in on them now. What little light was left in the sky was almost totally lost to the damp grey mist. The cold plucked at Danny's cheeks and made him cough. Squinted he managed to make out what looked like a large curved boulder on the floor to his right. Luke?

His friend was lying in a heap just in front of him,

crying and gently rocking back and forth. "I've broken my leg," he said. Then half screamed: "I can't feel it."

Danny bent to look.

"No, no, go away."

"You wanted me to look, didn't you?" Danny said, "How bad is it?"

Luke was silent for a moment. Now he was closer, Danny could see him slowly moving his hands over his lower legs. "Argh. It's broken." Luke said.

Danny held his shoulder. "Can you walk?" Luckily Danny could not see the stern awful stare Luke give him.

"What do you think?"

Danny shrugged. He'd never been good with sick people.

Luke was sobbing, his shoulders falling and raising. "It's broken… Oh…" His voice turned into a strangled cry of terror. "There's a bone sticking out. I bet there's blood everywhere. Am I going to die?"

Danny peered into the gloom.

"Help me. Don't just stand there watching me die."

Danny was looking at a dark blob on a dark hill. He couldn't see anything and hunted down in his pocket for his phone.

"What are you doing?" Luke asked.

"I can't find my phone."

There was a gasp. "There's no signal. What are you going to do with it? Take a blooming picture?"

"I need the torch part so I can see." Danny gave up

hunting for his phone and bent down to get closer to Luke's leg.

"Don't…" Luke yelled, "Don't touch it!"

"I'm looking." Danny gently moved his hand toward Luke's leg. He could feel the boy tense as he got closer. "Just let me see here…" Danny slowly moved the palm of his hand over Luke's shoe, past the laces, past the thicker part where the shoe met his sock, past the… Danny froze. There was something jagged sticking out of Luke's leg. He swallowed hard and peered as close as he could. There was a sharp bone-shape sticking right out of the top of Luke's ankle.

The next scream was louder - it belonged to Danny. When he got his breath back he managed to say: "It's broken all right. You've got a bone sticking out."

Luke sobbed again and wriggled his face away. "I'll never walk again."

Just then, the air was filled with a loud crack that made them both jump. Danny lurched to his feet and ran a few steps away before he realised that it was thunder and not an explosion. When he turned back, Luke had gone.

Gone. Danny paused. What's happening?

He spun around in the mist white darkness, hunting for his friend. This was weird. Were aliens out here abducting injured children? Would he be taken next?

There was a rustle of leaves behind him.

"Argh." That was Luke.

The two boys faced each other in the dying light.

"What are you doing creeping up on me like that?" Danny said. "You could have given me a heart attack…" He paused, a new thought had just struck him: "How come you're walking?"

Both boys bent down together, feeling and fumbling towards Luke's ankle. Luke stood up first, something pointy in his hand.

The bone had come out!

Danny gulped. "What have you done?"

Luke made a strange noise that sounded a little like a laugh. "It's the pencil," he said. "I think I left it down my sock when my leg was itching.

TWENTY-FIVE
ANOTHER FALL

IT WAS ALMOST TOTALLY dark now.

The two boys hadn't spoken for over half an hour. Luke had tried limping for a while, but even that didn't cheer Danny up. Meanwhile, Danny had been continuously mumbling quietly to himself: "A pencil... A pencil... No broken bones then... Just a blinking pencil..."

"It did hurt," Luke offered.

"It will."

They were stamping slowly through the heather. Danny was the one doing most of the stamping. Luke seemed to be feeling sorry for himself, but Danny couldn't tell. What he did know was that this idiot of an almost-friend had filled him full of terror.

"We'll laugh about it later." Luke offered.

Danny shook his head firmly. He'd realised that since they had been going uphill when they left the village, if they went downhill now they would have a better chance of finding someone. Anyone.

Every few minutes, Danny checked his phone in case it had started to get a signal. But it seemed as though the whole world of technology had deserted them.

And that, Danny knew, was his fault. In fact, even though he was still mad at Luke for the ridiculous pencil in the sock thing, he had to admit to himself that this whole mess was totally his own fault. There was no getting away from it. What had his sister said? Something about rushing in and not thinking. That was right. He'd rushed the map which put that old couple in danger. He wondered if they were still alright. They were only just able to walk about on the flat tarmac in town, what chance would they have out here. He felt as though he had instructed a small baby to play in the middle of the road.

Any tragedy that came upon anyone here was going to be his fault. There was only one thing for it. Danny decided he would never make any decisions ever again.

Luke, with his usual bad timing, chose that exact moment to ask: "What are we going to do?"

DANNY GULPED, swallowing back the dark thoughts. "I dunno'," he knew this was far from helpful. "We'll just keep walking, I guess."

"How long have we been out here?"

Danny sighed. Boy was this boy irritating at times. "Too long."

They had to get back down the mountain. That's all he knew. Get back, find the town, find home. Or at least get back to where there was a mobile phone signal so they could call for help. Someone needed to get proper help out here for the old couple. Trust me, he thought angrily. He'd messed up before, but that had usually been because George had pulled him into some unfortunate plan, but this was his own fault. He could hear his teachers and neighbours moaning; the words came loud and clear: Trust Danny James. Of course, by trust they meant don't trust. That type of label was hard to remove. More worryingly, of course, was what could be happening to Ray and Irene right now. He could easily imagine their frail hands gripping those walking sticks as they tried to make their way through the mist on the hillside, following a map that rather than lead them to safety would take them into danger.

IT was so dark now Danny couldn't even see his feet. Still, he moved on in front of Luke.

Going down was all that concerned him now. He knew they had to get down quickly, so every step had to be in that direction. The grassy ground was uneven, and at times he took a step that twisted his foot. He tried to walk more carefully, knowing that behind him Luke was probably stepping in the same places he chose. Just then his foot hit a new clump of grass, and he staggered sideways. As he half-fell, he moved his left leg to catch the firm ground and hold himself upright. But this didn't happen.

It seemed as though the ground had different ideas and it refused to be there when his foot came down to rest on it. Beneath him was only air. His foot, leg and presently all of Danny just moved down and down. He let out a cry and flung his arms wide. His left hand brushed past something that felt like Luke's coat, a momentary feel of hard nylon and a zip brushed his fingers. He tried to grab at it, but it was gone like a bird flying out of his grasp. There was a long moment as he tumbled downwards. A picture flashed into his mind of a white and blue china vase hurtling towards the floor. Then with a teeth-wrenching thud, something came up and struck him in the back. He felt all the air go out of his lungs and, for a moment, he was too stunned to do anything. He was a balloon that had been released without being tied, the air rushed out and only stopped when he was empty.

TWENTY-SIX

DON'T MOVE

HELEN WAS at the kitchen window again.

Everyone else was in the living room. Colin had lit the fire, and it was warm and cosy in there. Helen couldn't stay though. The windows in the living room looked out on to the back fields. Only the ones in the kitchen looked to the mountain.

Not that it mattered. With the kitchen light on, all she could see was a dark reflection of herself. Helen switched the under cupboard lights off and looked out. She could just make out the difference between the sky and the cold hard mountain.

There was a bucket on the floor in front of the sink where Colin had been trying to repair the tap. She pushed it to one side to lean closer to the glass. For a moment she imagined she saw a flicker of light down one side of the mountain and she moved closer. But then it became easy to see that the light path was a raindrop that had hit the window and was slowly running down.

Come home safely, she thought. Come home soon.

———

DARKNESS. Stone black silence.

A wheezing noise woke him, and Danny eventually realised that the noise was coming from his own lips.

He breathed deeply; there was no way he could speak. He had to fight hard to get the air back inside.

After a few slow breaths, Danny let his mind float over his body and tried to imagine how he might look. He felt like he had been broken into hundreds of parts. He imagined a leg way over in the distance, and he tried to move it. His head hurt. He thought about his back, which was a painful thought, so he moved on to something else. His mouth hurt. There was something warm running down his cheek like someone had tried to put hot soup into his mouth and missed. There was a smell too. A strong smell of rust. He knew that smell, and the feeling on his face. The hotness was blood, and the smell matched it.

Somewhere, he was bleeding.

Above him, he could hear a faint cry that sounded like someone calling his name.

Things went silent again.

Four years later… Or was it only a few seconds. Danny couldn't be sure; the sound came again.

"Danny… Danny…"

It sounded like an echo, like someone doing one of those fake echoes or shouting through a long pipe. He groaned and tried to move his head. Ah, that was a mistake. Lie still again. Let the world slow down, and the stars and whooshing noises come to a stop.

He paused and the world around him paused too. There was only the harsh hiss of his breathing. It sounded like Darth Vader.

That made him smile.

Danny slowly lifted his head again.

This time the head and the body stayed together, and the stars didn't swoop around and dance in front of his face. His neck ached, and he felt it with his right hand. Ah, he realised, he'd moved his arm. At least his arm was working. That gave him confidence. He felt around with his hand and managed to sit more upright.

Above him, someone shouted: "Don't move."

Well, that was bad timing, wasn't it? He needed to move, his bum and his legs were getting cold, and he was starting to lose the feeling in them.

"I'm ok." He shouted. Although he wasn't sure it was true, and, if he thought about it the words didn't even seem to make the right kind of noise.

"Don't move, are you alright?

Danny realised with surprise that he was pleased to hear Luke's voice. Even the dumb questions cheered him and took his mind away from his painful body.

"I'm okay. I think I just said that."

"You've fallen… I don't know what to do. This is bad."

Danny groaned. That's great, Luke. Stop panicking and tell me something useful. But he said only: "I know. Don't worry. We'll sort it out."

"But you've fallen down… a mine shaft."

What? Danny had a momentary shock. What had Luke said? His brain didn't want to register the idea. If he'd fallen down a hole that would be ok. Well, almost ok. But a vertical mine shaft was a different thing; it was the difference between going to Blackpool for the weekend and going to the moon.

Mine shafts were deep. They'd done a project about it in school; some lead mine-shafts were very deep. Had he fallen right to the bottom?

"Are you okay?"

"I was." Danny realised he hadn't said anything for a few seconds and Luke was getting even more anxious.

"I'm still here. Just thinking," Danny said. "I'm going to be okay. We are both going to be okay." As he said this, he desperately hoped it wouldn't turn out to be a lie. "But, Luke, you've got to help. I can't tell how far I've fallen."

Then he remembered his phone and hunted in his pocket. When he took the phone out, he could tell something was wrong. It seemed to be hollow, and the screen felt rougher than it normally did. Of course, he knew it. Broken. Useless.

Danny swore and pushed the ruined phone back in his pocket.

Just then something flickered above him. Luke had managed to sort himself out; it seemed he had come up with the same idea. He was shining his phone down the mine shaft.

The light was closer than Danny had expected. In fact, it looked like he could almost reach it.

Just above his head, now he listened carefully, he could hear Luke moving about.

"That's great," Danny shouted up. "I can see your phone. I'm not very far down after all. I might be able to work my way out."

He scrambled towards the light, pulling at the rough sides of the shaft. It felt more like a hole in the soil than a man-made mine shaft, and he wondered if Luke had made a mistake. His legs ached and felt weak, but he managed to get a foothold and push himself up. Another reach with his hands and the soil he had been holding onto changed into something else.

That's grass. I'm at the top.

He sighed with relief and managed to reach out a little further. As he did so, the grass turned into something warm and smooth. It was Luke's hand. And Danny found himself being helped out.

As he reached the very edge of the hole, Danny dropped down on to his bottom and pushed himself away from the edge by kicking with his feet. Finally safe, he let go of Luke and placed his hands flat on the ground. The cold damp grass beneath him felt strangely calming, he wanted to hug it. Then, his loving search of the welcome ground brought his arm into a patch of nettles, and he changed his mind.

Danny had his senses back. "I thought you called this a mine shaft?" he said, rubbing his nettled arm but not saying anything about it.

"It was a mine shaft. They filled most of them in about twenty years ago. There are loads of them on this hillside. Filled in, but the soil sinks away and leaves a deep hole."

"At least it's not a full shaft down to the mine."

"Oh no," Luke said calmly. "If you'd fallen that far you'd be dead."

TWENTY-SEVEN

AT LEAST IT'S NOT RAINING

A LITTLE WHILE later the two boys started to walk again. It was an awkward, limping walk for both of them. Luke's ankle still hurt whenever he put any weight on it. Danny's back, right leg and arm were sore. His head was pulsing, and he still saw bright star specks if he moved his neck too fast. It was far worse than when he fell out of the window just a few days ago.

They managed to hobble, one behind the other, slowly checking each step as best they could in the near total darkness. Luke's trainers had glow in the dark laces, and for a while, that seemed to help, but they were fading now. Danny's phone was useless. So, they decided, they would have to keep walking on the half-visible grey parts of the mountain. Avoid the darker blackness, he told himself, that's where the traps hide. They could be chunks of soft heather or thunderously deep drops that would fill your body with pain or, equally possibly, kill you. Every step was a lottery. Danny grinned to himself at the odd situation; he remembered that Luke had wanted to take part in a raffle. Well, he was now. You draw a ticket with every step and if you're lucky, you get another go. If your number comes up, that's the end.

With these lessons in mind, Danny and Luke tried to make headway downhill again.

"I can't see a thing," Danny groaned, after a while. "Can we use your mobile now? Do you have enough battery left?"

"Can't. I never set up a torch app on mine. I can put the screen on though." Luke did this, but the light was no better than a weak candle bulb.

"Find a blank screen," Danny wanted the phone. "This one's too dark."

It wasn't any help. The gloom just ate up any light the phone tried to give out. "I'll turn it off to save batteries - we will need to call home as soon as a signal comes back."

They walked on.

Luke's foot hit an awkward clump of grass, and he cried out in pain. "I can't keep doing this."

They stopped.

Danny took a few more painful steps forward. "Come on; I guess everyone's waiting for us at home. Keep going down. We can't go wrong."

They walked on in silence.

Danny was thinking hard. When he'd looked at

Luke's phone it was past midnight. Tuesday now, a dark black day. He wondered about whistling a little tune to keep himself happy. But his lips were too cold.

"We're going to be out here all night," he said solemnly. "We ought to find some shelter."

"The best shelter will be home."

It was far from easy walking. Danny hoped they weren't walking in circles. With each step, they came nearer home. But with each step, Danny was constantly reminded of the old couple.

"We've got to keep going. This can't get any worse." He tried to find something positive to say: "At least it's not raining."

Danny had been breathing so hard as they tried to make their way down the hillside that he had forgotten to listen. Now, as his breathing eased, he caught a new sound. The wind had suddenly changed, and a grumbling noise now reached them. A distant rumble that sounded like thunder.

A storm was coming!

TWENTY-EIGHT
LOSE THE LIGHT, GUYS

OVER THE LAST FEW MINUTES, the air had grown colder. The boys looked up in the direction of the thunder. It was a strange distant rumble that sounded more mechanical than natural.

Luke cocked his head to one side and listened hard. "That's an engine."

The sound was coming from higher up, beyond the mountain.

The odd engine noise grew louder, partially hidden in the howl of the wind it became a deep low buzzing.

"A helicopter," Danny shouted.

"They've come to save us…" Luke said. If there had been time, Danny would have had a stern word to say about the stupidity of this, but the boys were too engaged in trying to attract attention.

They started by shouting and waving their arms in

the air. At least, Luke managed to wave two. Danny settled for just waving one.

As the helicopter sound seemed to circle around and then grow more distant, Danny stopped trying to wave. "This isn't working," he said. "There's no chance of them seeing us down here."

Luke's hand grabbed at his shoulder. "Give me back my phone."

"What?" Danny complained, but he handed the phone to his friend.

Luke adjusted the phone, swung it upwards and started taking pictures of the black sky.

"The flash. That's brilliant!" Through the pain, Danny managed to change his face into something close to a smile.

The phone camera's flash fired repeatedly, giving the two boys an instant view of the white mist above and the dark earth around them. Danny imagined the flash brightly illuminating the clouds and attracting the helicopter pilot.

The helicopter sound seemed to close in on them almost immediately, but Luke continued firing the flash.

Then, after a few minutes, the flashes grew less rapid as the phone battery started to fade. Just as Luke paused to save battery, the helicopter engine was drowned out by a loudspeaker.

"We can see you." A calm voice boomed from the heavens. If it had been accompanied by thunder and lightning, it could have been the voice of God. "Lose the light, guys. We have night vision. We can see you," the strong voice continued. "We cannot land, but don't worry, we will get help to you. Stay where you are."

A bright light beamed down through the mist.

"We're okay. We'll stay here…" Danny shouted upwards, but he was certain the owner of the strong, calm voice wouldn't be able to hear him.

A moment later, the helicopter circled over them again. "Right, we're dropping supplies. We'll be back in a few minutes to winch you up. Okay? Flash your torch if you understand."

Luke stood gazing up into the clouds. Then, suddenly realising what they wanted he switched on his phone's camera. Danny had sat back on the damp grass, watching. His side ached now, and he was beginning to sense that his arm was badly hurt.

Danny could see Luke was still fiddling with the phone. "What's the problem?"

"I turned it off. It's taking ages to come on."

The sound of the helicopter rose again. "Are you okay down there? Flash your torch if you understand."

"Yes, yes…" Luke had managed to get the phone working, he lifted it to the sky and took a picture of the clouds - the flash burst out.

A few minutes later there was a fluttering sound, and a parcel dropped to the ground nearby. Luke limped and hopped towards it and found it was attached to a thick wire. There was a clip at the end.

He quickly unclipped it and stood back. The cable danced sideways and rose gently back up into the air.

Danny had not moved from his position on the grass, but he managed to see the cable lift into the clouds. It was like a tentacle from some friendly alien, retreating after leaving them a gift.

Luke dragged the parcel over to Danny, and the boys opened it. There was a small medical kit, a set of thin, silvery blankets that were surprisingly good at keeping them warm. However, the chocolate bars they found were the boy's favourite items.

"Using the flash was a brilliant idea, Luke," Danny said. His eyes were full of admiration and his mouth full of chocolate. The warm blanket and the sweet taste helped him feel more positive. In a sense, he had to admit; it was a good thing Luke had been there. Finally, he thought, he might be able to let that ridiculous 'pencil incident' go.

TWENTY-NINE
WAIT FOR THE PHONE

HELEN HAD POLISHED the kitchen table four times already and was wiping it again, her eyes on the kitchen clock. "It's nearly one in the morning."

Colin glanced up, "We should have sent William home long before this."

"He's waiting like we are."

"Should I call them?" Colin had the phone in his hand.

Helen sighed. She wanted to say yes, she wanted news. Where was Danny? Was he safe? And what about Luke? She thought these things, but she knew they couldn't phone. They'd been told to wait.

"No," she said. "We just have to wait for the phone to ring."

The phone rang.

Colin immediately dropped it onto the table. It skittered and spun away from his fingers. Both he and

Helen dove to grab it, but he caught it and put it to his ear. "Yes?"

Helen held her breath. In some ways, she preferred the news coming through Colin. They'd tell him, and he would tell her… She didn't think she would cope with hearing it directly.

Colin was saying. "A helicopter — yes — very dark — they did what?"

Helen watched his face. Was he smiling? She listened for phrases like: "Oh good, they're safe", or, "right, you have them, and they're coming home." But those words didn't come.

"Airlifted — hospital."

"No!" Helen's voice was mechanical, "What do they mean, hospital? Where? Are they alright?"

Taking a step away from the table, Colin waved at her to hold the questions.

Without waiting, she ran to the door and shouted across to the living room. William and Ellie were watching some news program on TV. She knew they would want to know about the phone call. "Ellie, William, We've got news. The boys are safe. They're going to the hospital."

The living-room door was thrown open, and Ellie dashed out. "Right, we'll get our coats." She called back into the room: "William, you phone your mum."

Colin came out of the kitchen. "They're okay. They may have a few sprains and bruises. But they are okay."

"They were lucky."

Ellie jumped up with excitement. "Come on," she called as William caught up with them in the hallway. "Let's go and see them."

William had his phone in his hand. "I'll get my mum and dad to meet us at the hospital."

They were dashing out of the house when Ellie said, "Which hospital?"

Helen looked at Colin for an answer.

Colin looked back, thought for a second and then said, "The county hospital. They said it was the closest with a helicopter pad."

Helen quivered at the words 'Helicopter pad', it made everything sound so serious. "But where is that hospital?"

They all waited as though the answer would just appear by magic. A moment later, William came out of the house. "The County Hospital? Yes, I can show you the way?"

Helen sighed and ran back to Colin's car. "Ellie, can you lock up the house, quickly? William, you get in the front—"

She pulled at the door, but it didn't open.

Colin waved the key fob at her. "That's what I'm doing," he said. "The doors are all stuck."

"What?"

"Don't worry." Colin repeatedly pressed the button on the remote key fob. He held the key fob high in the air. He held it low to the ground. He held it directly against the side of the car. Then he started the process all over again.

Helen, watching all this, was anxiously twisting her wedding ring around her finger. This was taking too long. She felt she needed to scream. Eventually, she gave in to the feeling, but managed to draw the scream back to more of a shout: "Colin!"

They all looked at her.

"Leave it. Leave your car. We'll take mine."

She pulled her keys out of her bag, and they all ran around Colin's car and started getting into Helen's. Ellie and her dad were clambering into the back but found the seats were piled up with papers.

When they complained, Helen looked over her shoulder from the driver's seat. "I forgot those, just drop them in the boot. Quickly."

A moment later they were all back in the car. Helen calmed herself, and they set off for the hospital.

THIRTY
BE CAREFUL HERE

DANNY, with a heavily bandaged shoulder and a blue cast on his wrist, returned home the next morning. His sister was keen to help him out of the car. His mum had parked as close to the house as possible, but Danny had to hobble around his dad's car and a mechanic's dirty green truck. The mechanic was looking through the passenger window of the car.

Danny wondered what the problem was, but other matters had to come first.

"Be careful here, it's a high step." That was Ellie advising him on how to get up the step into the house. He didn't say anything, but she must have known that he'd been up and down that step dozens of times. She was being kind, and that was a plus.

There were sounds of more people inside, and Danny wondered who it was. He felt a little sore and unsteady. Since leaving the hospital, he had been hoping to return to a nice quiet house. Maybe some time to himself with the TV, or an Xbox game.

Last night, the helicopter had taken him and Luke to the emergency ward of the hospital. And that had been the noisiest, most uncomfortable time of his life. Luke had been able to go home after only a quick check-up. But it didn't work out so well for Danny. He had stayed in a ward for what they called 'overnight observation'. He wasn't sure who was doing the observing since he hardly saw any nurses or doctors until the following morning. But, he did feel much better now. The painkillers they had given him were working well.

His thoughts were interrupted by Luke, who was standing just inside the hallway giggling at him like some silly, ticklish girl. Helen was pushing hard at the door. "Why won't this open all the way? I want to make it easy for you to get inside." She looked behind the door. "What's this?"

Even in his pain-killed state of calmness, Danny gulped. The boxes, oh no!

"Are these yours?"

"I was going to move them but with all the…"

His mum smiled. "Never mind, dear. We can sort it another day. Can you get in, it's a little narrow here."

Happy that his mum didn't seem to mind the boxes in the hall, Danny squeezed inside without any complaints.

Luke was there. He was in Danny's face: 100%

Luke. Questions, questions, questions. Danny had to tell him about the X-rays, the tests on his lungs, the ones on his eyes, ears and throat. Yes, his wrist was in a cast. Yes, he knew he was wearing a protective collar. It turned out he had a minor fracture of his collar-bone and a clean break of his left wrist. Who would have guessed that? He never really felt any pain in his wrist.

Of course, it would have to be his left hand, wouldn't it? No missing writing on his first week in school. Mind you; he had already decided to tell the new teachers that he was left-handed. He hoped he would earn lots of sympathy too.

There was a pause in the questions during which Danny managed to get a little further into the house. Then Luke remembered something important he wanted to say: "The helicopter was fantastic! I liked landing on the hospital roof. That whoosh and the roar of the engine. I thought my ears were going to—" Luke stopped to interrupt himself. "But, I really liked going up in the harness. So fast."

"I don't remember that." Danny was almost at the end of the hallway now.

"You were tied to a stretcher."

"They'd given me something to make me sleepy; I don't remember."

"You were all tied down. You looked like a captured criminal."

That made Danny laugh, and with a genuine sense

of warmth, he finally found space to say. "It's good to see you, Luke."

They moved past the hall and into the kitchen. Colin met him at the door. He gripped his son's shoulder (his good one). "You're looking better, son. A night in the hospital has done you good."

"I feel okay, a bit wobbly."

"You go into the kitchen and sit down. There are some surprises in there." Colin let his shoulder go and moved past him. "I've just got to sort my car out. It's a complete mess. That's why I didn't come to pick you up from the hospital. I've been waiting for this mechanic." He headed for the front door.

Danny was puzzled, but he went into the kitchen. Immediately, the full force of the heating hit him in the face. His cheeks felt like they were burning. Is this the surprise? Dad's had the heating on?

No, there was more. There was a strange atmosphere. The room felt busy, it was filled with people and warmth - the kind of warmth that came from happiness, not radiators. It made Danny think of Christmas, everyone jolly for their own reasons. But some of this was a little hazy. Luke ran past and sat down with a woman, Danny guessed this was Luke's mum. He was going to go over and say, 'hello', when a familiar figure sitting at the kitchen table caught his attention.

THIRTY-ONE

ARE YOU ALRIGHT?

IRENE WAVED AT HIM. "We're both here, all fine," she said. "My Ray's just gone to the toilet. He's 87, you know."

Danny walked steadily across the room. William was by the window showing Ellie something on his phone, but he looked up and smiled as Danny passed.

Limping a little, he came close to the table.

Irene looked him up and down and smiled warmly. "Do you need to borrow my sticks?"

He laughed.

"Are you alright?"

"I could do with the window open if I'm honest."

There was a glint in Irene's eyes: "You, honest?" It sounded like a question, but he couldn't be sure. She rapidly covered it up by adding "You're doing really well. You're a hero, you know."

Danny squirmed at that. He didn't feel much like a

hero. "But what about the walk? You didn't go up the——"

"Mountain. No, dear. We looked at the map and decided it looked a bit complicated for us. So we went to the cafe for a drink and a sit-down. Anyhow, lad, thank you for going out to find us. Even if we weren't there." She said. "I knew you were a good 'en." Again, Danny felt uncomfortable, he wasn't sure he deserved that title either, but he was pleased she thought it was a possibility.

Irene looked across to where Luke was sitting. "This morning, Ray sees the paper, and there's a story all about you two in it. About you being on the mountain overnight. We had to come and see you."

"I should give you your money back."

"No, you shouldn't. You might need it."

Just then Ray and Colin came into the room together. They were deep in conversation. As they got close to Danny, he saw Ray hand his dad a card and say something about house repairs.

Colin looked at the card and showed it to Danny.

Joe Lockhart

Plumber and joiner

"That's my son," Ray tapped his finger on the card. "He's a good worker. He'll see you right." He looked around the kitchen, pointed to the sink with pipes sticking out and the bucket in front of it. "He'll sort that for you in any case."

"Oh, that is useful. Thank you." Colin moved his gaze to Danny. "It's all happening today, isn't it?" It was one of those silly things adults say.

Danny felt something touch his one good hand. When he looked down, Irene was passing him a bundle of wool. "I made this for you. Well, I made it for you to give to your mum."

Danny looked at the woollen thing, not sure what it was. He unwrapped it carefully in case the wool itself wasn't the gift but only a wrapper for something inside. He was worried it would break. He needn't have been concerned, as the wool opened, he could clearly see what it was. A blue and green scarf. Irene had been knitting. "I've always enjoyed a good knit," she said. The smile in her eyes told Danny that she knew full well this was a comical thing to say.

He shook his head.

But Irene insisted and pushed the scarf back into his hands. "Go on, take it. She'll love it, I promise."

Danny knew he still had to have a conversation with his mum about presents, so he decided to put the scarf out of the way and save it for her birthday. He thanked Irene again and hid the scarf in a drawer.

Before he could do anything else his mum came over, she ruffled his hair. Normally, he would have pulled away, but he stayed where he was.

"I'm sorry, Mum," he couldn't hold back the tears now.

His mum held him close. "It's okay, it's okay," she said. "You know Danny," she murmured close to his ear. "You've done some silly things in the past. And you did some silly things over the past few days too."

Danny mumbled through tears, "I'm sorry for breaking the vase."

"Don't worry. You're safe now. Everybody's safe, they…" she stopped, pulled away from him and frowned. "The vase? What vase?"

Danny gulped, there was no escape. It had to be done now. He told her what had happened to the ornament a few days earlier. Her reply shocked him.

She laughed.

"You do know where I got that vase, don't you?"

"Yes, Mum. I'm sorry. I know it was special. I remember you wrapped it in bubble paper and put it in a box, inside another box to keep it safe."

"To keep it safe, Yes, dear. I did." His mum carried on stroking his hair. "Do you remember Garden Street Infants, your first school?"

Danny nodded.

"I got that vase in a jumble sale there. It was 50p."

"What?"

"Your dad broke it in… well, in 2011 I think. He knocked it off a shelf with his guitar." She looked across at Colin as she spoke.

Danny looked too.

TRUST DANNY JAMES   175

"He glued it together, of course. But it was a bit fragile, so I packed it carefully when we moved."

"It wasn't precious then."

"Only in your head," she said. "But if you want to buy me another you can."

"They're £45."

Helen looked at him in surprise, then laughed. "Don't buy me one - get me a voucher for a haircut instead."

Danny snivelled, wiped his nose and gave a little laugh.

"What I'm most proud of, Danny. Is that you tried really hard to put things right. I'm not talking about the vase. I'm talking about——"

"Yes, Mum. I know." Danny sniffed.

She gave him a gentle hug around his waist. "Hey, I've just thought. I already have the best Birthday present possible… You, safely back."

Danny had to wipe his nose again.

———

THERE WAS a knock at the back door.

Colin opened it, and the car mechanic stepped into the kitchen, he was wearing gloves and holding a scrap of cardboard like a tray. The cardboard held what looked like three pieces of twisted fudge. He showed them to Colin, and they spoke urgently together. Danny was fascinated.

The car mechanic left with the cardboard and the fudge, and Colin turned around. The atmosphere in the room was changing. Everyone had fallen silent. They were all as fascinated as Danny.

Colin seemed to be tremendously pleased about something. "Ah, now we know what's wrong with my car." He started to walk around the kitchen. All eyes followed him.

"What's the matter?" Luke whispered to Danny. But there wasn't time for a reply. It's all happening today, Danny thought.

Colin walked over and looked at his wife. "It seems there's some foul-smelling sticky liquid inside the cigarette lighter."

He moved his gaze to Ellie, "All the circuits are burnt out, and the car needs a complete overhaul."

Next, he smiled broadly at Irene and Ray, and said cheerfully, "They're going to tow my car to the garage, it may be there for three days."

These all seemed like bad things, but he was stating them in a constantly cheerful way.

Danny was confused.

Then Colin stopped gazing around and looked firmly at Danny and Luke. Everyone else in the room did the same. "You two. How did cat wee get inside my cigarette lighter?"

Luke looked at the floor, and Danny seemed to be searching the ceiling for an answer.

Colin snapped his fingers. They both looked at him.

When he stared back, he was only looking at Danny. "And…" he said, drawing his next words out slowly. "Can you explain how cat poo got all over the driver's seat?"

Helen gasped in surprise, "Cat poo?"

Colin turned to look at her. "Exactly!"

He turned back.

But Danny had gone.

EXTRA

Thank you for reading 'Trust Danny James'.

I hope you enjoyed meeting Danny as much as I enjoyed writing about him. If you did, please leave a review so other readers can find out about him too.

I'm sure you will also love finding out what happens to him next.

You can read the first chapter of this next book, **"Look Out Danny James"**, right now... (turn the page)!

There's more about Danny, his family and friends on my website: maxjdelaney.com

Max

LOOK OUT DANNY JAMES

—

Chapter 1

—

Danny had never been summoned to the head teacher's office before.

He had been in trouble on a few occasions at his last school, but this was a totally new experience. He shifted uneasily on the wooden bench, feeling the smooth surface of the polished wood with his fingers. The bench had clearly been there for many years; Danny imagined that hundreds of different bottoms had made use of it. Most of the bottoms probably belonged to worried children.

Waiting outside the head teacher's room was probably a frightening time for many. Not for Danny though, he felt confident and cheerful. He had only been in the school a few months since moving to the town from London. He was certain he hadn't done anything wrong. The headteacher probably wanted to thank him for something, or give him a special report.

Danny looked idly at the wall next to him. The familiar pictures he'd seen on the days when he visited with his mum were still there. But now he noticed a few certificates in dark wooden frames, the same dark wood as the bench.

He stood to inspect them more closely.

They were mainly photographs or old cream and gold certificates. The photos all showed people looking very smart in their school uniform.

Danny sighed and looked down at his own tie and a dark red jumper. He still found this new uniform awkward after the junior school's sports tops. The jumper pulled up around his shoulders, the tie always made a lumpy mess at the front. Some other kids he knew, wore their tie sticking out of the top of their jumper, but this made them look like they had a horse-tail on their neck.

Danny grinned at the thought as he looked at one of the framed photographs. It showed a rather large girl riding a rather small horse. In the corner of the photo was a cutting from a newspaper. Apparently, this girl had done something wonderful at a horse event.

Danny wasn't impressed.

The next framed photograph was labelled 'School Champion'. It was an image of an older boy. He seemed to be incredibly happy as he grinned out from behind the glass. The boy was holding a huge silver trophy and had obviously done something totally wonderful. The glass reflected Danny's own face too. He moved back to stand so that his face lined up with the other boy's. It didn't quite work. Even standing on tiptoe, he couldn't get his eyes and chin to match. Danny shrugged, he clearly wasn't going to win a trophy, not even as a reflection.

He moved on to look at the next few frames. There was the captain of the swimming team shaking hands with someone in a fancy hat, and a boy called Griff Ogden-Evans had won a maths competition a few years ago.

Danny could do that. He liked maths.

But, he had to admit to himself that no matter what he did he would never get his picture on the wall outside the head teacher's office.

The next frame held a certificate, issued to the school by someone called Estyn. Most of it seemed to be in Welsh and Danny was still trying to find any English words when he heard a door open behind him.

"Ah, Danny." Mr Henderson smiled down at him.

Although he had seen the head teacher every day since starting school in September, Danny was always surprised by his appearance.

Mr Henderson had Harry Potter-style glasses, a tightly curled white beard and a flop of white hair on the top of his head. He always wore a brightly coloured bow tie, the colour of which changed every day.

Today, Henderson's bow tie was a dark, ruby red. Danny felt he looked like a mix between a well-groomed Father Christmas and a prize-winning poodle.

Henderson twirled his glasses in one hand before pressing them smartly back on his face. Then he stood to one side and waved Danny into his office.

Danny stepped inside, and his shoes immediately sank into a soft carpet. The spongy softness reminded him of the teacher's beard for a moment, and he had to hide a quick smile. Henderson smelled of furniture polish, and his office did too.

There was wood panelling under the window and a low polished table. Next to this was a dark leather sofa, its large knobbly feet digging deeply into the same dark blue carpet. The sofa was empty except for two small red cushions. Danny couldn't remember when he had seen a sofa as neat and tidy as this. The one at home was permanently covered in things. No one could sit on it because it was usually full of his mum's books or his sister's clothes. If it wasn't her clothes, then it was Ellie herself, draped over the arms while she painted her nails or (more usually) gazed openmouthed at her boyfriend's text messages.

Danny carried on looking around the room until he was directed to sit in a nearby chair. Henderson, or Happy Henderson as Danny had learned he was called by some of the older children in school, wore a permanent smile on his face. There was a gap in his curly beard and Danny could see that he was smiling now.

As Danny lowered himself into the waiting chair, he realised that, like the rest of the room, the chair was extremely comfortable. From here, he thought, it would be easy to imagine the whole world was a lovely warm, comfortable place.

On the wall behind the teacher, there was a photo-graph of a pale sailboat bobbing on gentle grey water. At the sight of this Danny relaxed even more.

The photo reminded him of his own sailboat. For as long as he could remember, he had always had an imaginary sailboat. Danny had no idea where his made-up boat had come from, or why he would some-times think about it. But just occasionally, an image of a sailboat would pop into his mind. Most often, it was a pale blue boat with a pristine white sail on a lovely calm sea. At other times though, when he was in trouble, his mind would show him an image of a rough sea and a boat heaving dangerously about in the crashing waters.

Right now, Danny's mind was totally calm and untroubled.

"Now, Danny." Henderson broke into his thoughts. The teacher was moving to a metal swivel chair behind his desk. He was too big for the seat, and he knocked the desk as he sat down. A pot of pens rattled.

Henderson reached out a large flat hand to stop the jiggling pot. Then he leant to one side and lifted some-thing out of his desk drawer.

"I need to talk to you about this."

Danny looked at Henderson's '*this*' and felt suddenly worried.

Look Out Danny James
is available now from Amazon.

Printed in Great Britain
by Amazon